A BREATH OF FRESH AIR

Life has a strange way of dealing with conflicts

FOREWORD: *by Paul Carufe*

So, you think you know someone?

During the course of your life, there are certain people you meet and with whom you just 'hit it off'; Ilee is one such person. When Ilee and I met in college twenty-six years ago, the only thing we had in common was our love of basketball. He came from the urban streets of New York City, and I was the complete opposite, having been raised in a small town in the Hudson Valley.

In the fall of 1989, we became college roommates and developed an awesome friendship, and it wasn't long before I invited him to come and see where I grew up. It was quite a humorous affair: I took him to a local watering hole and together we chuckled at how the locals would stare. Conversely, when he would bring me down to the city area, I would get looks of confusion from the locals - but again, we didn't care, because we spoke the international language of basketball.

Fast forward twenty-three years: Ilee and I had graduated college and started families and careers, but had continued to remain in touch. He had relocated to Florida and I had remained in New York. One day in the Summer of 2012, I received a call from my friend, stating that he needed a break from paradise. He informed me that he needed to see some mountainous terrain and feel a cooler breeze upon his face - and he was quite serious, because a week later, he was at my house. We played some golf, put the boat out on the Hudson River, caught up with old classmates and laughed as if we had never left our college team house.

So, where am I going with this?

Well, one night during his visit, my wife Sarah, Ilee and I sat around the fire pit and talked. He opened up about some of his childhood experiences and we were blown away. He told us about a unique program that he was a part of called the ***Fresh Air Fund***. Sarah and I had never heard of it. He went on to describe how it had made such an enormous impact on his life and the way he viewed the world. We were intrigued. After Ilee's departure, Sarah and I began researching the Fresh Air Fund program hoping that we could make such a huge difference in someone's life.

Then it happened.

We became Fresh Air Fund host parents and for the past three years, have had a chance to connect with an awesome young man who has become part of our family. We have been able to enrich our lives as well as his, as we get to experience the joys of innocence while teaching him to fish, jet ski, mountain hike, etc. I cannot thank Ilee enough for being such a great friend in my life and sharing such intimate details of his past. Hopefully I can have the same positive effect on my Fresh Air Fund child's life as Ilee's family had on his. My friend taught me the importance of paying it forward in life.

A meeting became a friendship; a friendship became a brotherhood; a brotherhood became a way of life.

PREFACE

Unlike the deformed, stunted trees that emerge from the contaminated soils of the big city, trees in suburban communities grow tall and strong. They are nourished by the maternal hand of nature and supremely protected by the inhabitants of the neighborhoods they oversee. One serves as a thrifty umbrella that covers the ungodly secrets that are cemented within the concrete crevices, whilst the latter is carefully planted, to repeatedly serve the few who find solace in her beauty and eat from her bare hands.

Israel has found this to be a truth early in life. He and his best childhood friend walk a tumultuous line between success and failure, fantasy and reality, prey and predation. Utilizing quick wits and visions of life in a brave new world, they maneuver through the metropolis, interacting with past and present allies, invisible bullies and the gatekeeper of an overzealous imagination. At odds with life as they know it versus life as it should be, they are trapped within a constant tug of war.

But life has a strange way of dealing with conflicts.

CHAPTER 1:
WELCOME HOME

A well-groomed pair of black Gucci suede loafers, size twelve, lay flat on the floor of the recently waxed auditorium stage. Resting in them were the feet of a man who had long wrestled with the taunting of self-doubt and insecurity since the early days of his childhood. Unbeknownst to his rambunctious audience was the fact that even as successful as he appeared to be in his custom Indochino blue vested suit, aqua colored dress shirt with matching presidential silk tie and *"bling-bling"* accessories, he was battling with a certain degree of uncertainty. Invisible to the sea of naked eyes belonging to his awe-inspired onlookers was the daunting presence of skepticism seated snugly on his left side, and ambiguity seated closely to his right. The embedded irony masquerading within the details of this encrypted conflict is that this same gentleman had been commissioned to stand in front of a graduating high school senior class and verbally coax their limited focus towards setting goals, chasing lofty dreams and ignoring the toxic poisons hidden within negative self-discussion.

With the piercing rays of the afternoon sun relentlessly tormenting the faded tint on the windows and steadily increasing the temperature inside the building, Izzy sat upright, trying to keep his composure. While staring into the majestic sea of hopefuls, he would occasionally ruffle his note papers just enough to disrupt their comprehensive order. An unforgiving nervous twitch he had carried with him from childhood chose this exact moment to resurrect itself, and began directing his lower limbs to repeatedly collide against the legs of the gray fold-up chair he was occupying. If he allowed this increasing onslaught of anxiety to get the best of him right in that moment, then this particular battle waged within his omnipresent war would ultimately result in a loss.

Sitting on that stage under those exceedingly hot, illuminating lights for an extended period of time would cause anyone to break into a sweat, but it was much worst for Izzy; he seemed to be approaching the level of spontaneous combustion. His nervous energy had petitioned heavily for perspiration to rear its colorless exterior and attack the dryness within the folds of his armpits. Shortly thereafter, running along the razor-sharp edge of his recently-groomed hairline were tiny beads of liquid fear. The steady formation of small waterways throughout his thick head of hair began to swell and as if the dam had sprung a leak, down his face ran the tears of an unhappy scalp.

I can identify with these familiar components of Izzy's struggle; I know them all too well. As his best friend and confidant, I am privy not only to the extreme highs, but also the excessive low periods that this man has experienced throughout his tumultuous life. Whether the situation is bleak or at the peak of ecstasy, he and I are usually the two remaining entities amongst all the vanishing hoopla and the slowly-fading spotlights. Most of the time, he adheres to my conservative advice, but when he decides to rev up the engine past the level of flamboyant, he ends up in places and situations that are hazardous to him physically - and sometimes emotionally. So, when I saw the beads of sweat aligning themselves along his forehead ready to make a run for it, I gently whispered in his ear:

"PAUSE!

Now take a deep breath, count to ten, then let it go."

As elementary as my instructions to him may sound at times, they are usually just what the doctor ordered. I guess my voice is comforting enough to go in one ear and remain there long enough for Izzy's brain to process the message and right the ship.

Izzy began to regain control of himself. He reached into the inside jacket pocket and withdrew a pearl-white colored handkerchief, which was embroidered with his initials in black, and patted the excess moisture from his face. The sporadically oscillating leaf fan located just a few feet above his seat gave him short bursts of relief, but the outstretched grasp of Hades was steadily closing in. With only three of the five blades still intact, the vaulted cooling system on-stage was producing just enough of a breeze on top of his heated skull to cause the appearance of a smothered flame. Maybe I should have advised him to remove his jacket, but to us, the image of professionalism was always about the entire package. First impressions are extremely powerful and we understood that the look of having "*made it*" was just as important to these kids as the positive messages written upon those disorganized pages in his clutch.

"Ladies and Gentlemen, we are extremely fortunate to have one of our own return to the neighborhood and share his life experiences and wisdom with us. He, too, was once where you are seated and with the fuel of a huge imagination and enough belief in himself that he could accomplish anything he set his mind to, I am proud to introduce to you our very own success story, Israel Lemhi."

Just as our hostess completed her introduction and the applause began to pour in from the crowd, Izzy arose from his grey seat of solitude and broke into a wide-mouthed grin. He received an ovation fit for a wrongly-exiled king who had been exonerated and returned home to reclaim his throne. Plastered all over his face was the heartfelt appreciation and joy of an overwhelmed schoolboy. I truly believe that at that very moment, he was reaching back and reconnecting to a time in his life when he sat in those very same seats and hoped for the return of a role model with whom he could positively identify. It was a beautiful and emotional experience to witness; I was extremely happy for him.

Izzy folded his arms and took a bow. He returned to an upright position with a glow of unshakable confidence. No longer filled with a gallon of anxieties, he took a firm step forward towards the podium and without any warning, the unthinkable occurred. Due to the previous puddle of fears that were excreted from his body, the soles of his designer shoes became unglued from the surface of the shiny floor.

I couldn't believe what my eyes was showing me, nor the immobilizing feeling of despair that cocooned my body. From a perched position upon that stage, I sprang into action. I began sending frantic messages to all of Izzy's life-long bodyguards to break his fall. Out from his body flew his left arm, followed by his right. Both were trying to find a solid object to grasp onto, but when gravity arrests you and makes a decision to summon your backside, it's always an abrupt introduction between flesh and floor.

I knew Izzy's misstep was going to be painful and because of our unique relationship, I realized that I had to experience it with him. His legs were all but perpendicular to the floor and his torso about 30 degrees south. The papers that were originally held firmly within his clutch had been tossed skyward and were now slowly falling back towards his body like thrown confetti. I witnessed his rotated torso collide first, followed by the crushing blow of his skull, which rendered him unconscious. Everyone in the auditorium was stunned. The roaring applause of the crowd quickly became replaced with the silent echoes of stressful confusion. They stood in awe and watched as the words of one of their heroes fell from the sky and eerily blanketed his body – much like the white sheet that is draped over a corpse.

"Call 9-1-1!" shouted the host. "Hurry, someone dial *9-1-1!"*

I must admit that I began to feel kind of light-headed myself. Maybe through all of the excitement and chaos, coupled with the heat exposure, eating only a banana for breakfast probably wasn't the smartest of ideas. I decided to lay next to Izzy's motionless body. I reached out and clenched the hand of my best friend. With my head snuggled close to his ear, I whispered, *"Don't worry buddy! Everything will be alright! You are home and we amongst friends!"* Almost immediately, I noticed tears pouring out from underneath both of Izzy's closed eyelids and onto my cheek. His lips were twitching, but I struggled to decipher what was being said.

"Dad...

Daddy...

Daddy, don't!

Please... Daddy, stop...!"

"*What is it, Izzy? What is it?*" I asked.

Finally, through all the loud silence and organized chaos, I heard the words:

 "*NO, DADDY! STOP! PLEASE DON'T ... PLEASE DON'T HIT MOMMY ANYMORE!"*

CHAPTER 2:
Memory Lane

The back of the ambulance was cold. The responding Paramedics were performing their duties just as they had learned in EMS class, and after witnessing some glaring communication break-downs, I wondered exactly how many of them had cheated on their final exams. Uncertainty was beginning to take a back seat to fear, as I witnessed my best friend struggle to maintain consciousness.

"DON'T JUST STAND THERE!

BEAT ON HIS CHEST!

POUR SOME WATER ON HIS FACE!

DO SOMETHING!"

I was shouting at the top of my lungs, but it didn't seem to do any good. The only feedback I was receiving seemed to come in the form of a *smokey-white* mist that hovered around my lips every time I exhaled. By this point, fear was in full bloom, taking over the bench seat next to me and spreading like an uncontrollable ameba. I was feeling despair ascending from my chest, traveling up into my nostrils and opening the doors to my cerebral control room. My hands were shaking as if I was the lead in a high-stakes dice game and the dried up tears around my eyes made me look as if I had been hit in the face with a box of chalk. Usually, when people find themselves in such a precarious predicament with nowhere to run or no one to call for help, they end up on bended knee, having a one-way conversation with an invisible entity that hopefully has enough power to alter their situation in a more positive way. After that initial thought, I made the decision to act upon faith, so I formed a "*crouching tiger*" position, closed my eyes and knocked hard on God's heavenly door:

"God, I know we haven't talked in a while and I know there are some things that I need to work on to better myself, but I come to you today not asking for myself, but for my best friend. Please step in and lay your healing hands on the health and wellbeing of this man. He is absolutely well-deserving of your generous gift of life and liberty! Thank you Lord!"

I wasn't sure where the words were coming from at that particular moment, but I knew they were sincere. Amazingly, my anxieties began to subdue once I had gathered myself and returned to a normal seated position. My adrenaline levels, which had been astronomically high just seconds prior to my request, were descending back to a state of heightened alert and the fear that had been relentlessly suffocating the room for what seemed like forever, began to unwittingly relinquish its hold- allowing me to breathe again.

I reached out to hold Izzy's hand. I understood that he couldn't verbalize the emotions that were flooding though his mind and body, but the short contractions of his fingers towards his palm let me know that he was aware of my presence. I placed my left hand on top of his, which was already clenched in my right hand, and patted it twice.

"I'm here, my friend, and nothing could prevent me from doing so. Everything will be fine. Relax, we are headed towards help."

I spewed those words into the air at a decibel level barely heard above a whisper. It was hard to tell which one of us was on the receiving end of the reassurance I was offering, but I do recall the pupils of my eyes returning from an upward position.

As I sat back and closed my eyes, I began patrolling the outer lanes of reality; desperately searching for an opening in the traffic through which to hop. Once inside the middle lane, I could look to my left and see reality speeding by - and to my right, fantasy was just a couple of meters behind. Soon, the roar of the sirens was fading and the muffled sound of my beating heart could be heard in the silence. The external *"noise"* that always accompanies chaos had subdued itself and given way to an eerie calmness, not unlike the eye of a terrible storm. My current thoughts of the future began morphing into flashbacks from the past and before I could shut down the mental intrusions, I was high-stepping down memory lane.

A dusty grey and red bus carrying a multi-cultural set of passengers and bellowing out dark toxic smoke from its rear, ran northwest alongside the Manhattan-bound 59th Street Bridge, making a right turn onto 21st street, then a left onto 41st avenue, followed by a wide right turn - just missing a black wrought-iron fence - and onto Vernon Blvd. Tugging on the royal blue cord that ran the length of the bus served as a mechanism which alerted the driver that passengers were ready to exit at the next scheduled stop. After initiating the brakes to bring the motorized behemoth to a complete stop and sliding the door lever towards the right, you could hear the sound of compressed air being released from its confines. A four-step descent from the stairwell and onto the pavement positioned you directly beneath four red, white and gray smoke stacks of the iconic Con Edison power plant. The sight of these four majestic pillars, coupled with the constant sound of tires crossing a grated roadway stemming from the bridge always made us feel safe at home – similar to how the sounds of the waves hitting the rocky sands of the beach on Coney Island did for the gang in the cult-movie classic *The Warriors*. A city within a city was the best analogy I had ever heard to describe our demonic Garden of Eden. This was the place where we lived, loved and learned about life amongst 96 reddish-brown sister-buildings.

During the 1970s and '80s, this was our stomping ground. With six families housed on every floor and six floors in every building, you can only imagine how many personalities we had to maneuver our way through on a daily basis. To an unsuspecting outsider, the never-ending stream of people constantly running in different directions probably seemed like an out-of-control human infestation. Our blessings came in the form of overactive imaginations and natural gifts of creativity, which enhanced our playground interactions and excited our levels of competitiveness. We played schoolyard games like *Skelly*, *Ring-a-lario*, *Stickball* with the chalked out box etched on the building for the strike zone, and *Taps* off the chin-up bar. We took aluminum food cans from the trash, cut out both sides and used them as a funnel to spray water from the illegally operated fire hydrants onto cars passing through - whether they were due for a wash or not. We knuckled up aimlessly amongst ourselves, mainly over adolescent pride and territorial bravado, but an outsider didn't stand a chance of experiencing a victory. Most of our parents knew one another so our *"beefs"* were mostly squashed at the executive level.

...AND BASKETBALL???

As a whole, we loved and embraced the game of Basketball, much in the same way as America loves its apple pie. To us, Basketball served as a way of expression, a way for us to come together as a community and a means to garner respect and adoration amongst our peers. It was a divine vehicle that some had used to propel themselves to fame and fortune and it allowed timid little guys, like we were, to dream big and follow in the footsteps of those who came before us. All we had to do was make a decision to work hard at becoming one of the best in the neighborhood, garner enough courage to compete, then dribble our way right out of the Matrix!

CHAPTER 3:
Friend or Foe

Izzy and I first met in 1976. It was at a time when life was much different than it is today. 1-800 hotlines and anti-bullying campaigns were not the popular household remedies that they are today. Almost all domestic disputes were settled within the confines of the home and whatever occurred behind closed doors and sealed windows would never see the light of day; it was sheer defiance to put your family's business out into the street.

In the cafeteria of our school, the rows of white-topped, silver-legged tables housed the classes of kids designated for that period of lunch and recess. It was the very first day of being in a new school with new classmates and I just happened to be sitting across from a skinny little boy with a half-mooned afro. He seemed to be in a heightened state of awareness, signified by his need to keep constant watch over both shoulders. I gave him the *homeboy head raise,* which silently sent a *"hello"* signal to his internal antenna. He squared his eyes at me and politely gestured a return nod. Amongst all the ferocious conversations taking place at the same time, we began to carve out our own space and start an allegiance of words.

"So, how do you like it so far?" I asked.

He shrugged both shoulders and replied:

"It's alright I guess. It's not like we got a choice."

"Yeah, our teacher seems to be a little crazy, though. Do you see how she rolls her eyes out into space when she talks? That's not normal."

"That's funny! I did think she was a little out there, but you gotta be a little crazy to be around here all day every day!"

We continued on with our introduction, and through further conversation uncovered that we were both children of divorced parents and we lived within close proximity of each other. We were too young to hang out together after school because we both were limited to the confines of our respective blocks. Most of the time there were more than enough things to do on your own block, but when kids decide to be adventurous, the mind shields the body from those invisible boundaries. Our conversation led us to exchanging phone numbers and we both breathed a sigh of relief that we had found someone with whom we could relate and ease our transition into a new environment.

RING!!! RING!!! RING!!!

The bell signaling the end of lunch and recess had put an end to our conversation. It was now time to gather our belongings, empty our lunch trays and head back up into the vaulted dungeons for the remaining lessons of the day. I picked up my black-and-white Mead, marbled-print composition notebook, unraveled my legs from the protection of the table and diverted my attention towards lining up with my fellow classmates. I took a quick glance behind me to see where my new friend was, only to find him lying on the floor with his feet raised and resting on the benched seats. The laughter of the other children seemed to trouble Izzy more than the fall; I could tell from the way his head cowered, -seemingly trapped under the weight of disgust and embarrassment. I raced over to help my new-found friend to his feet and discovered that his untied shoelaces were entangled with the legs of the lunch table. From that moment on, Izzy and I became close companions.

A few days later, I received a call and immediately came to the conclusion that my favorite classmate had a mind unlike any of the other kids. His was always in *"go-mode"* and his memory rivalled that of a high-speed processor.

"I need your help with something I am working on" he blurted.

"Sure! What is it?"

In a cunning but firm voice, he replied, *"Operation Get-Back!"*

"Operation Get-Back? What are you talking about?"

"Don't worry! I got it all figured out. I just need a little help. Will you help me or not?"

"Yeah. I'll help you. What do you need me to do?"

After learning the details of Operation *Get-Back*, I realized that my friend was not just another kid that roamed around the playground aimlessly. This young man was unusually smart - a thinker, a planner, a coordinator. What he lacked in muscle and mass, he more than made up for with his brain. I decided that it was more advantageous to remain friends with someone like that than become an adversary. He explained how he had been observing who sat where during the school lunch period. He stated how a certain group of boys would bully their way through the crowd in an attempt to sit next to the popular girls, and together they would make fun of the rest of our classmates. He went on to say that the popular girls loved the attention and that is why the bully boys continued to flex their muscle and treat the other students like crap. He thought that since they wanted to be together...let them ***BE TOGETHER!***

The next day I came to class with a grin that would not subside; the recess period could not come soon enough as I anticipated the employment of *Operation Get-Back*. I looked across our crowded classroom to make eye contact with Izzy, but he wouldn't look my way. He didn't smirk, he wouldn't chuckle, and he couldn't even acknowledge my *giddiness*! There was no change in his demeanor all day. This kid was seriously in character and to him, anything outside of the norm would have cast light where there would be certain doubt.

A few hours later, we began our decent towards the cafeteria. In two distinct lines, boys on the left and girls on the right, we marched in an orderly fashion down three circular flights of stairs. Once we reached the doors of the cafeteria, I knew it wouldn't be long before all hell was going to break loose. Our class began filling in the three sets of tables that were aligned together to accommodate our group. The lunch period went about its usual chaotic routine, and exactly as Izzy had explained, the last kid received his tray and returned to his seat just before the bully boys began their ritual of jockeying towards the middle of the table, surrounding the popular girls.

I sat anxiously across the table, watching as my friend proceeded to casually eat his grilled cheese sandwich and waited for some type of signal. Two bites into the ingestion of my own sandwich, I felt a tug at my right pants leg. I was a bit startled, but quickly realized who it was once I cut my eyes left to where my friend was sitting. He tugged at my pants again and I slowly slid myself below the off-white tabletop and into the realm of slouchy tube socks and colorful plastic *Jelly* sandals. Altogether, we manipulated the shoelaces of about ten students. Not only did we unravel and re-tie shoelaces to the legs of the table, we strategically placed slightly-opened ketchup and mustard packets between the legs of the *"populars"*. Izzy's plan was so detailed that he even knew which kids leapt from their benched seats without first removing their legs from under the table. It was extremely hard for me to keep my composure and finish the job without chuckling. In my peripheral vision, I could see Izzy cut his eyes, urging me to say stay focused.

After the job was complete, I maneuvered back to my seat and motioned the girl sitting beside me to stay quiet. Izzy crawled to the other end of the table, where the teachers were sitting. There was a kid who was being reprimanded for something he did earlier that day, so he wasn't allowed to mingle with the rest of the class, but he was one of the kids that Izzy had in his sights. Just as Izzy had unraveled his knotted laces and coiled them to the steel leg of the table, a man leapt down the stairwell and landed in front of our table – inches from where Izzy was crawling.

"Who the hell hit my son? Was it you?" he screamed.

The startled teachers sitting at the edge of the table all drew back in sheer fright. The intended target was our Arts and Crafts teacher, who had, at that moment, been on the microphone in the middle of making an announcement.

"*It was her, Daddy!*" shouted a little boy who, along with his mother, followed the man into the crowded cafeteria.

The parents of this young boy rushed towards the teacher and attacked her with vicious intent. They beat her with swift kicks and closed fists, knocking her to the ground and dislodging her teeth in the scuffle.

SHEER PANDEMONIUM ERUPTED.

All of the kids in that lunchroom were yelling and screaming as if for their own lives. Our bully boys tried to make a run for the other end of the room, only to find that their knees would strike the underside of the table and their feet would be tied to one another. The popular girls attempted the same escape, but found themselves in a similar fate with a slight twist. Once they fell back to their seats the packets of condiments exploded onto their clothing and for the remainder of the day they endured damp red and yellow stains in their crotch areas.

The police finally arrived and arrested the two parents, and the boy was ultimately removed from the school, but *Operation Get-Back* was no doubt a complete success. No one ever discovered who orchestrated it.

The chaos provided by the infuriated parents created the perfect camouflage. Everyone was so flabbergasted by the commotion that no one focused on the table incident.

For a few moments, Izzy stared intently in my direction and took a slow bite of his sandwich. The gleam in his eye was one of content and immense satisfaction. He whispered something very softly through semi-closed lips, but I was uncertain of what he said exactly. To this day, I never asked him about it, but I always believed it was...

"NOW, YOU CAN LAUGH!"

CHAPTER 4:
SCARE TACTICS

The more we hung out together, the stronger our bond became. Izzy and I began sharing bits and pieces about our home life, our dreams and what we would like to change if we could. Occasionally, Izzy would say something that would make my jaw drop and my eyes water, but not wanting him to feel uncomfortable, I'd sometimes exaggerate my own encounters just a bit. I was becoming more and more intrigued with the inner workings of my friend's thoughts, and the passions that fueled his heartbeat. The complexities of his life and the people governing it provided a stark contrast to the person I was getting to know, but I also realized that his persona was a direct result of all he had experienced up to that point.

One day after school, Izzy and I had begun to walk home, when we noticed the blackness that was overtaking the clouds above. We began to pick up our pace at the sound of the rumblings above; I had always been told that when GOD clears his throat, you'd better run for shelter! We made it as far as the Chinese Restaurant before the downpour showered the landscape.

"We can make it to my house and you can call home from there," Izzy shouted, trying to be heard above the weather.

"Ok, but will your mom be angry?"

"No. I'll call her at work and let her know."

We clenched our backpacks as tight as a caught football and ran towards Izzy's house as if we were dodging defenders trying to enter the end zone. Once we reached the top floor of the building, I was led towards the back corner apartment on the right, underneath the number six and adjacent to the garbage incinerator. Izzy put the key in the door and turned it counterclockwise. The mechanism inside the metal door unlocked and when the door was swung open, I knew I was walking into a world of further discovery.

"Yo! You wanna play hoops?" Izzy asked.

"How are we gonna play hoops in the rain?" I replied.

"You gotta be creative. Check this out. Watch me and learn!"

Izzy grabbed a brown wire hanger from his mom's closet and bent the hooked part at a ninety degree angle. He then manipulated the enclosed triangular portion with his hands. When he was through, the hanger was no longer adept at shouldering the weight of an article of clothing. It had been transformed from an uneventful hanging tool into a lively and exciting circular mini-hoop equipped with a fastener that would fit in between the door closure. From the top drawer in his room he grabbed a white pair of gym socks, which we used as a ball. We began jumping and playing like we were mini kangaroos and before you knew it, we had gone through two hours. I was getting a little tired and the game was fairly close. I was ready to concede the win but Izzy wouldn't accept it. He wanted to beat me. He started to increase his physical play as if we were playing for our lives.

"I quit!" I said.

"What? Stop being soft! That's not how you get to play with the big boys!"

"But I don't want to play with the big boys! ...And since when did you become so worried about playing with the big boys?"

"Well, I was watching the tournament on the block the other day and Jixx was playing. He was killing them out there. Everyone was screaming his name and they were fans for real! I was like yeah, that's my brother!"

The excitement in Izzy's eyes was magical. Whenever he spoke about Jixx, it was coming from a place of intense love. There was no mistaking his feelings for his *brother-from-another-mother*. Jixx was not Izzy's biological brother, but to him, that was irrelevant. Jixx was actually the neighbor's son, who stood about 6'4", with dark black hair that he wore in a mini afro, and a body kept in military shape. Izzy was Jixx' protégé and both relished in their respective position. In his eyes, Jixx was what he aspired to be, so whatever Jixx was into, his apprentice couldn't wait to jump right in with both feet.

I can remember a time when we were riding our bicycles behind the four man group that Jixx was navigating. Izzy's bicycle caught a flat tire and Jixx decided to fix it at the gas station across the other side of the gigantic, two-directional, four-laned roadway that bordered the entrance of our neighborhood. We had been warned not to cross this street due to its dangerous nature, but Jixx assured us it would be alright, so we all went and bought a flat patch from the five and dime store, obtained a book of matches and wove our way through the sea of cars, ultimately reaching the repair station. Once there, the older boys pulled the slim, black inner tube from the inside of the back wheel, pumped it up, and found the tear that needed to be repaired. With us standing closely in the background, Jixx glued the patch over the torn section of the inner tube, then applied the lit match to the glue in an attempt to seal them together. He waived the match several times to extinguish the flame, then casually discarded it over his right shoulder. No one noticed that the flame was still alight, when it latched onto the frills of Izzy's bellbottom jeans. At the sight of his blazing leg, everyone jumped to a frenzy of hitting and throwing things, trying to put out the fire. Izzy began frantically jumping around and beating his pants leg with his fragile little hands. Jixx grabbed a water bucket and doused the flaming pants until it looked as if Izzy had been swimming fully-clothed. We came up with the brilliant idea of taking the pants to the neighborhood Laundromat to dry them and rid them of any incriminating evidence. After the pact had been made to keep this to ourselves, we continued our playful day well into the illumination of the streetlights.

There was one slight problem.

Overnight, Izzy's three fingers on his right hand had blistered up from his palm to the tips of his fingernails. The yellow pus that had begun oozing from his hand scared him and his mom so much that he was taken to the neighborhood clinic the following day. She knew that the story he gave where he touched the oven while it was hot was a lie. After hours of questioning and extensive examinations by the physicians, Izzy's mom entered the room begging and pleading with him to tell her and the doctors what really happened. Izzy felt so bound to the pact made with Jixx that *snitching* was not an option. Up until the time he saw tears flowing from his mother's beautiful brown eyes, he had been as steadfast as a soldier. Suddenly the rules had been changed, as he could sense that this wasn't going to be the normal shut-up-and-let-it-pass scenario. She finally connected with his heart and explained to him that the doctors had assumed that he was being physically abused at home. A report was being filed for the state to investigate and if they concluded foul behavior, he would be removed from the residence. There was no one Izzy loved more than his mom, and with this new set of circumstances, he finally came clean and told the truth.

"It's getting late. I better head home."

"Ok. I'll see you in the morning. Same place as usual right?"

"Yep!"

I picked up my backpack and headed for the front door. Gliding past an open window, I noticed that the aftermath of the pouring rain had become nothing more than a gentle breeze of mist. We exchanged our big boy handshake and as I reached out my hand to grasp the doorknob, it took a violent turn in the opposite direction. The big metal door swung inward, and through the rectangular doorway walked a tall, dark man with a brown leather jacket and matching hat. He glanced in my direction, followed by a frown that appeared to be an attempt to merge his eyebrows into one.

"And you are...? He says.

"I am...about to leave" I replied.

I respectfully told him who I was as I put on my knapsack full of school books and hurried towards the steps. I took one last look over my shoulder and watched as Izzy slowly closed the door. The look on his face was one I had not witnessed yet. It narrated an entirely different side to a story that I had not been privy to. I overheard the action of the locking mechanism, and my heart sank all the way to my knees with the realization that I may have just met the boogeyman. I hurled myself down twelve flights of stairs, opened the heavy steel front door of the building and ran all the way home.

CHAPTER 5:
UNCLE AL

It was a hot and humid Friday evening and I found myself as an overnight guest at Izzy's house. The tin-foiled Jiffy popcorn pan had a few kernels of corn remaining and the 13-inch colorless television was now displaying a hypnotic snowy picture. Izzy's cousin Len was in the backroom whispering sweet nothings into the phone to one of his adoring female fans. He volunteered to stand guard and watch over us while Izzy's mom was out. His generous offer was not done because he cared about us; there was an underlying motive of food, beer and open phone lines that garnered his attention.

I watered my eyes with a yawn and elongated stretch from the short nap I took only to find Izzy, pretzel-bent on the sofa across from me, sound asleep. The movie we were so desperately dying to see crept by us sometime during the night and it would be another month or so before it would be aired again. I wasn't going to wake Izzy, but I was being lazy and didn't want to get up to turn the television off.

"Izzy! Izzy! Wake up! Wake up!"

I shook him hard enough that I startled him. He jumped to his feet in a daze, with one eye still shut and began mumbling as he walked to the television and tried to adjust the wire hanger that had been propped into the antenna to help bring about a clearer picture.

"Izzy! Izzy! Open your eyes! We missed the movie."

"Ah! Not again!" mumbles Izzy. *"I guess it's just not for us to see. Where is....?"*

The latch from the front door began to turn counterclockwise.

Our eyes immediately became fixated upon the round door handle, and like a slow-motion scene from a turbulent movie thriller, in walked the heinous villain dragging his damsel-in-distress behind him.

In a fit of anguish, Izzy yelled out, ***"WHAT HAPPENED?"***

The tall man who wore the leather hat and matching jacket replied, ***"She fell!"***

Izzy leapt out from underneath the blanket he was covered with and took hold of the unidentified woman. She was much bigger than he was at that time, so I decided to lend a helping hand. Frantically, we struggled our way down the narrow hallway, past the two bedrooms where Len was still on the phone, and made our way towards the bathroom. Izzy flipped on the light switch and all we could see was a river of blood gushing from the nose and mouth of this unidentified woman.

"Mommy! Mommy! Are you alright?" cried Izzy.

No response.

I stood in the doorway of the washroom with a puzzling but frightful look on my face. I was trying to make sense of what was occurring and was equally stunned at how Izzy responded in such a rapid fashion. There was no hesitation in his efforts to revive the woman, who I had come to realize was his mother. I stood frozen in complete amazement as I watched him sit her upright on the white porcelain toilet, before simultaneously raising her head and pinching her nostrils to help stop the blood flow. With a free right hand, he maneuvered close enough to garner a red and white wash cloth, then soaked it with cool water. He gently rubbed it across her face and in doing so, began to erase the aftermath of an earlier occurrence that had gone bad. I couldn't help but think to myself... maybe this is not the first time.

"Everything is gonna be alright mommy! Here, sit up straight and let me take off your shoes! I'm gonna go and get an ice bag for the swelling around your nose and some Vaseline for your lips! Don't worry! I'll be right back!"

Izzy left the room.

I couldn't turn away from what I had just witnessed and my feline curiosity forced me to go in and take a closer look. I took a forward step, then a long bend from the waist. My eyes squinted ever so slightly as I attempted to focus in on the facial details that would link her and Izzy together. A brown-skinned woman with a slim frame and high cheekbones, which had originally been covered in bloodstains, began to become unmasked and revealed a more natural "girl-next-door" familiarity. I inched a little closer to see if she was still breathing and then I clutched her right wrist to see if there was a pulse. I am not sure what made me do that other than my need to assist my friend, coupled with having watched one too many episodes of *Quincy MD*. When I released her limp wrist from the pinched position of my home-made medical exam, I also took some of the blood with me and disturbingly transferred it to my pants leg.

"*Yuck!*" I whispered.

Suddenly, I felt a clasping sensation encompassing my right arm and when I gazed upon her face again, I found a startling pair of bloodshot brown eyes piercing through the air and starring right back at me.

"*Owww! Get off me!*" I yelled skirmishly.

Like a knock-off version of a Marvel comic superhero, Izzy swooped in from my blind side and wrestled me away from further danger. He grabbed her left wrist, which was as stiff as if stuck in a muscle contraction, and then began peeling away her clawing fingernails, which were lodged deep into my skin.

"Ma, let him go! This is my buddy from school. He is spending the night...remember?"

Almost instantaneously, the pressure from her Vulcan death grip was demoted to a calm handshake and mimed apology. Together, we guided her from the awkward position she was sitting in, across the frizzy neutral-colored rug and onto the sofa, where we were pretending to watch a movie.

"Is she gonna be alright?" I asked.

"Yeah! She'll be okay in the morning. This is what happens when they hang out with their unforgiving friend Al!"

"Who is Al?"

"Al Hall is a wannabe member of my family who shows up only to wreak havoc and cause chaos. I hate him for what he does and what he stands for and my folks just won't stop him from visiting. They allow him to come and go as he pleases and within an hour or so of his arrival, all hell breaks loose."

During his verbal description of Al Hall, Izzy walked over to the linen closet and grabbed a blanket to put over his mom's motionless body. His eyes were swelled with water, but he wouldn't allow himself to cry.

Instead, he diligently continued to walk around the apartment making sure the door was locked, the windows were shut and his mom was comfortable. As we headed towards his bedroom, he told me that he made a promise to himself to always stay clear from Al Hall.

"He is nothing but a bad influence and every time he shows up, there is trouble. I can't wait to get outta here so I don't have to deal with this stuff. Now you see why I'll never attend any school function that require parents to come. I know that if I was to bring up the possibility of attending a function with my parents, there would be a strong possibility that Al would come too!"

Izzy reached up and pulled the dingy white string to shut off the lights. We heard the creaking of the heavy front door opening and shutting for the final time that evening as Len left the apartment. The moonlight that crept through the slight crack in the doorway of Izzy's room gave us just enough contrast to see the silhouette of the *tall man* glide by. Due to the introduction of Al Hall into my life, I didn't get much sleep that night for fear that the new and improved boogeyman would show up and violently ingest me. For years, I continued to look over my shoulder and keep one eye out for the immeasurable menacing force that Al represented. The more time that passed, the more maniacal his legend grew. It wasn't until we were headed to high school that I realized that Al was none other than our bottle-

dwelling fiend, "Al K. Hall".

CHAPTER 6:
A BREATH OF FRESH AIR

Positioned in the unwelcoming caboose of what could only be described as a frigid mini-clinic, I felt confronted by the reality of today's events. All sense of feeling had now left my hands, and in an attempt to keep them from freezing, I decided to sit on them. I wasn't really sure what to make of my decision, though, because eventually my hands warmed up, but the extra pounds I had packed on due to months of inactivity were preventing the blood from reaching my hands and fingers; the result was a sensation similar to freezer burn. Slowly but surely, as I once again regained my sense of touch and mental acuity, I began to hear the high-pitched screams of the sirens.

I anxiously wanted to know the answer to the most annoying travel question… *"Are we there yet?"* but I knew it would only irritate everyone. Unlike a New York City cab driver, I was betting that the Ambulance driver was not running on any profit meter. We were streaking through traffic as fast as possible without creating any further incidents, but as always, when it's you or your family being transported, even the best of the best is just not good enough.

"How do you know each other?" asked one of the paramedics.

"We're best friends since elementary school" I replied.

"What kind of friends…."

"Not THAT kind of friends!"

We all exhaled an uncomfortable chuckle, which eased the tension of the surrounding situation for a moment. Izzy continued to remain motionless, but I could tell that he was eavesdropping on what was being said. I began to spew out all of his positive qualities; I wanted him to have a reason to fight for his life. I also wanted his caregivers to know that they were not just handling another Joe Schmo. Their motionless cargo was undoubtedly priceless in so many ways, on so many levels to so many people.

"Does your friend smoke?"

"No!"

"What about abusive drinking or drug use?"

"Nope. Neither. Why do you ask?"

"He has a slight wheeze in his breathing."

"Oh, he is an asthmatic."

The paramedics began to prepare a solution that would help open Izzy's breathing tubes. My confidence in their level of competence began to increase rapidly. I was glad that they were being extremely attentive to what could have possibly become a tragic oversight. I watched as the solution was integrated into the breathing apparatus and applied to his face. The deep inhalation of chemicals passing to and from the 'gas mask' exuded a distinct odor and a recurring cloud of smoke reminiscent to the steam that escapes from underneath the manhole covers on a New York City street.

Ironically, almost every adult involved in Izzy's growing up years were uncontrollable chain smokers. I'm certain that this environment created more harm for the little boy who couldn't breathe, but it was something he had to get used to. It seemed as if it was a daily ritual that he would run to the corner store to pick up 2 packs of cigarettes – Salem Lights in the green and white pack for mom and Marlboro regular in the red and white pack for the Tall Man. Both would light up consistently and the barrage of nicotine smoke would seep into everything it encountered and overpower anything intended to counteract its smell.

Izzy's clothing would reek of those odors every morning he entered our classroom. It was so intense, that he was always accused of being a smoker himself. What I have learned over the years is that once you have been subjected to a certain lifestyle or culture over a length of time, you either succumb to the pressure of joining the crowd, you totally rebel against it or you develop ways to coexist...and Izzy is no different. Armed with a yellow Proventil inhaler to help him breathe, a red bag of Wise barbecue potato chips and an orange soda, my friend would always show up to fifth grade homeroom out of breath and extremely charged. He would silently attempt to enter class through the back door, gasping for air after sprinting to beat the bell, but his heavy wheeze and tobacco odor trail always gave him away.

Izzy claimed he was born an asthmatic. He said that having the condition was limiting at times and when a full-blown attack occurred, it was like drowning without any water. Similar to standing behind a passenger bus that has just pulled away from the curb and emitting a billow of black smoke into your face, the amount of time before taking your next breath of clean air could seem like an eternity. I would always be cautious of our prolonged aerobic activities such as running, swimming and sports that would create an immediate need for him to consume extra air. Somehow, Izzy learned to survive with it and not let it become debilitating, but it was always in the front of my mind. The only time I let go of the stronghold was when he would do his annual 3-week disappearing act.

Every year, since the age of five, Izzy would be removed from our inner city oasis and find himself hundreds of miles away in a suburb which he later nicknamed Eden. His mom, who was only in her mid-twenties at the time, made an invaluable decision to place her young son in a program which allowed him opportunities to see life outside of their five-borough fishbowl. This program, The Fresh Air Fund, was unique and way ahead of its time. Izzy would always say to me:

"If it wasn't for the Fresh Air Fund, my outlook on life would be totally different than it is today. Not only did I see, hear, smell and taste different things - I was exposed to a way of life and a way of thinking that challenged almost all of my beliefs; I learned first-hand to see things from other people's perspectives and to think about the consequences of my decisions and actions."

Then, to break the serious vibe, he would add:

"You know, I really don't know if my mom was thinking outside of the box and realizing what she was doing when she enrolled me in this program. Was she so enamored with the potential of what this could do to better my life, that it gave her enough courage to send her baby boy hundreds of miles away to a place that she had never been and to people she had never seen, or did she just want a break from having me around for the Summer? You know how a young kid can sometimes become a burden on the social scene for young parents..."

We would always laugh afterwards, but the truth of the matter was that the effects of that one decision had changed the course of generations within their family. The magnitude of his mom's herculean resolution stretched his brain, challenged the parameters set before him and laid the foundation for a frail little boy with a breathing disability to feel confident enough not just to survive, but to compete and win at the game of life. He swore it was the best gift she had ever given him outside the gift of life.

Like clockwork, the beginning of every summer would make Izzy giddy and bursting at the seams with anticipation. The school year would soon be coming to an end and his annual trip to Eden was now on the radar. He knew that he would be shopping for new summer clothing and getting extra attention as a going-away present. These things made him feel good and I was happy to see him smiling, but also sad to see him leave.

"Too bad you can't come with me"

"I know! "

"Can you ride with us to the bus station?"

"Penn- Station? Yeah, buddy."

"Cool! Now you can see that big bus with the picture of the grey dog painted on the side of it. It's humungous and it even has a bathroom on it. Last year, a girl got sick during the five-hour trip and I saw her covering her mouth trying to hold in her food but with all the movement in the rear of the

bus, she lost control and the result was a new tie dye pattern on this boy's shirt. It wasn't funny at first, but at least there was a bathroom onboard to clean some of it up. The only bad part is if you are sitting in the back and someone takes a dump and doesn't flush right away, you have to hold your breath, knock on the door and tell them to FLUSH!"

"Ewww! That's nasty!"

"Yeah, but funny!"

I accompanied Izzy and his mom during their shopping spree. I didn't buy anything in the stores, but I more than made up for it at the corner hot dog stand they frequented in downtown Brooklyn. Clean socks, underwear and tee shirts were the first items on the list of necessities. Izzy would be trying to fill the cart with all the fancy, name-brand designer wear - which was relevant in his world, but was irrelevant in Eden. So, as fast as he would throw it in the steel rolling basket, his mom would place it back on the shelf. In Eden, the children had only one agenda and that was: *FUN FOR THE DAY*. Labels and branding were vehicles that encouraged limitations and exclusivity. Dirt did not discriminate against anyone and all clothing that was within its realm was susceptible to being pounced on.

Later that evening, I stayed and ate dinner with Izzy and his family. Everyone seemed to be in great spirits and full of laughs. I did notice an empty chair, which I presumed was reserved for the Tall Man - but he wasn't home and I was glad. I figured he was hanging out and having fun with Al Hall. It was cool to me because without them, there seemed to be a loving aura that roamed throughout that apartment and I was being swept up in it. Izzy went into some of the bumbling tales of his previous Eden adventures and kept us laughing for hours. We stayed up way past the intended bed time, as the stories became more insightful and the lessons learned more poignant. Izzy's bags were all packed and lined up by the heavy metal front door. It was becoming a reality that very shortly, I was going to be without my friend for an entire month. When all your emotions become confused and your brain takes a few seconds off from work, you uncontrollably blurt out untimely things like:

"Wouldn't it be so crazy if you overslept and missed the bus?!"

Gleeful facial expressions suddenly turned sour, and the piercing looks headed in my direction were numbing. I didn't mean to say anything to clear the room, nor did I want to stop the 'music', but I guess it was for the better as it was late and Izzy needed to be up early to reach his destination on time. I removed my right knee from its place on the padded seat cushion and placed the chair I was leaning on firmly on the ground. I took a step back to push it under the table, when I felt someone standing behind me. I knew it wasn't Izzy or his mom, as they were directly in my line of sight. By process of elimination, I took an educated guess of who it was shadowing me. I felt sheepishly scared, helpless and trapped. I excused myself and followed Izzy into the back bedroom. My hands were shaking and my heart was pounding feverishly.

After a few moments, when all was quiet and the lights were turned out for the night, I meaningfully looked over at Izzy and asked him,

"What is the **REAL** *reason why you are so anxious to get away from here?"*

He began to respond, but found the correct words a bit more difficult to spew than expected. I could sense that he was being protective of his speech and my innocence, so I eased him out of that awkward silence by posing a more pleasant question:

"What kinds of things do you do when you are with your other family that keep you wanting more?"

I felt that he deserved to have a back door opened for him to escape from the verbal trap in which I had placed him. I began to feel deep in my heart that he was a torn specimen; a bird with one broken wing; a prince without a kingdom to rule, but when he gets outside of the castle, his God-given light illuminates everything and everyone around him and his level of stress subsides significantly. Izzy found it a bit easier to describe the things that excited his senses of adventure and curiosity. I listened attentively until the sound of his voice forced me to tilt my head backwards and make indentations in the fluffy white pillow that accompanied me on the bed. My eyelids immediately became attracted to each other, decided to meet and soon all I could do was breathe in and breathe out in total darkness.

CHAPTER 7: D.I.P.U.T.S

RING!!! RING!!!

"Hello! Who is this?"

"It's Izzy! Can you talk?"

"Yeah, wassup?"

"Funniest thing happened at the pool today. I told you how we are having swimming lessons in the morning, to the park for a couple hours to play, then receive our return tickets to the afternoon pool session...right?"

"Yeah, AND...?"

"Well, a group of us were having so much fun at the park that we decided to hang together at the pool. I was doing all kinds of splash dives and cannonballs..."

"What is a cannonball?"

"Never mind! Anyway, we were having so much fun eating candy and swimming; we all decided to lie on our towels and work on our tans. Since I was born with a permanent one already, I refused the offer of tanning lotion being put on me. Soon we all fell asleep. I began having that dream again about the sun coming closer and colliding with the earth and it woke me up in panic mode. The first thing I saw was a bunch of legs and feet and

mine were different. I screamed out at the top of my lungs "Oh snap!"

Everyone rushed to my side and was asking me what the problem was and

after taking a few breaths and calming my nerves, I looked back at them and

said …I'M BLACK!"

Izzy would call me every week with stories about the good times he

was having with his *other* friends and family. He would elaborate on the

places they would go, people they would meet and exotic encounters that

captivated his mind. I was really happy that my best friend was getting to

do all of these marvelous things and have all of these wonderful

experiences. When he would call, I would prop myself underneath the tan-

colored, wall-mounted phone in our house and be swept away with the

enthusiasm and passion which he displayed within his story telling. He made

me feel like I was right there sharing those unique experiences with him.

"Do me a favor?" he asked.

"Okay. What is it?"

"Would you please ride by my home and see if my mother needs

anything?"

"Yeah, I will do that. What's the matter?" Izzy's attitude seemed to

become a bit somber.

"Nothing. I have just been having a lil' trouble sleeping at night. It's tough at times when I don't speak to her, but I guess she deserves some time to herself."

"Don't worry, dude. I will check on her. It's not a problem."

Izzy seemed to need that reassurance. It was the beginning of what eventually became a life-long mind intervention. Whenever adversity crept into the paradigm and altered the steady electrical currents of his brain, my timely insertion of words and calming phrases shifted the imbalance back to a manageable plateau.

"I appreciate you, dude. You are definitely my best friend."

Seconds later, I heard a click and then his voice was replaced by a dial tone. My connection to my brother from another mother had been severed, and he was off to partake in another adventure. I pouted for a while, but relished the day when he would return from where I refer to as 'Never-Never-Land', because I knew it was somewhere I would never get to see.

As the weeks passed and the circled date on the calendar drew closer, I began preparing myself to learn more about where Izzy had been, so that I could talk to him with a bit more knowledge. I would look through the green and white encyclopedia that rested underneath the coffee table of our home, trying to gather facts and other pertinent information of where my buddy had been. One thing I knew for sure was that when he returned home, he would be surrounded by all those who had missed him and wanted to reconnect with him, but because most of them had never left the confines of this "red brick city" in which we lived, their belief systems and imaginations were as inadequate as those who swore the world was flat.

One person in particular, Harland, was always overly aggressive towards Izzy and I. He was a few years older than we were and took every opportunity to belittle our existence and toss negativity into our positive circle of friends. I knew jealousy and envy were manipulating his thought patterns and erroneous behaviors, but Izzy was blinded by hatred and disgust. Harland was a dark-skinned guy with a very slim build, who didn't have much going for him and it seemed as if he liked it that way. He stood about six feet three inches tall, weighed about 185 pounds, and wore his hair all over his head in styles that were fitting for the most popular television tough guys. He kept his attire to a minimum, with pullover hoodies and stonewash denim jeans that fell onto a dingy pair of wheat-colored construction boots. Izzy always tried to limit his interaction, but it seemed as though Harland was infatuated with making life tough for him.

I rode my bike over to Izzy's building and leaned it against the grey, chain-linked fence. I looked over my left shoulder and then my right, to make certain that no one was scoping me out to learn my combination to the bike lock. One click, two spins and three tough tugs later, I was headed toward the heavy metal door that led into Izzy's apartment building. With my hands glued to the sides of my face like blinders, I pressed my face against the thick glass that was decoratively carved into the front door. It is a ritual that is practiced before entering any building because of the potential dangers that could await you on the other side of the handle. Through the glass slits in the door I could see two men standing in front of the squared mailboxes and blocking the entrance into the neighboring stairwell. Their demonstrative body language and hand gestures toward each other proved to me that they were in a deep conversation, until one of them noticed my distorted features through the glass and signaled for the other to turn around. Unfortunately for me, the second person in the stairwell turned out to be Harland. As he completed his pirouette, I noticed that across his t-shirt written in big bold white letters were the initials:

D.I.P.U.T.S.

Harland wore the six-lettered t-shirt with extreme pride and satisfaction. I chuckled under my breath a bit before composing myself and giving him the familiar neighborhood head raise.

"Come in here young buck. Explain to this guy what the letters on my chest represent and how much I inspire you weak-minded fools."

I looked at him with a bit of frustration and a belly full of anxiety. I was not his personal media guide and I certainly didn't like the fact that he was trying to punk me in front of an audience. My ultimate goal was to get to Izzy's house, so to avoid any conflict I bit my tongue and replied:

"Divine Intervention Propels Us To Succeed".

Through tightly-clenched teeth, I began to spew out an enormous fabrication about how this lazy, uneducated, drug-selling, insensitive, dragon-breath, bean-pole continued to inspire us to do the right things and excel in life. With a confused look, much like that of a deer caught in headlights, I could see what the third person in that hallway was thinking:

"How ironic is this?"

Released from the midst of my tormentor, I turned around and catapulted my body up the flight of stairs and into the elevator. I pushed the command button to take me to the top floor and maneuvered myself in the corner opposite some smelly brown waste which laid on the floor. I found solace in Izzy's voice as I could hear him reminding me that all I had to do was hold a mirror up in front of Harland and allow him to really read what the letters meant that were pressed so prevalently upon his crisp black shirt. Thanks to the quick wit of my best buddy, we had perpetuated an everlasting way to deal with Harland and all his inappropriate antics.

CHAPTER 8:
Faith vs. Doubt

The only thing I could focus on through all the commotion occurring in the hospital wing was the steady blip on the screen of Izzy's heart monitor. His chest cavity continued to swell with help from the pure oxygen being fed to him through the plastic tubing that had been inserted into his nostrils, and the mask covering his face. I began talking to him about the many things we had scheduled within the next few weeks. My eyes began scouring the room, looking for a place to play. Hanging on the wall directly across from me was a poem which read:

Faith vs. Doubt

Doubt sees the obstacles.

Faith sees the way.

Doubt sees the darkest night.

Faith sees the day.

Doubt dreads to take a step.

Faith soars on high.

Doubt questions ' who believes '?

Faith answers ' I '.

-Fawzia Zie

After reading the message numerous times and really internalizing its meaning, I started to experience a sudden quiver in my upper lip and irritation in both of my eyes. I began thinking about how infectious Izzy's personality was and how life to him was all about how you make others feel once you have come into contact with them. Moments before we entered the auditorium on that fateful day, our conversation was fixed upon Paul Williams, the World Class boxer who had suffered the life-altering motorcycle accident. Izzy said that most people would write him off as a 'should've, would've, could've', but Paul's biggest asset was his remarkable positive attitude and his ability to touch and inspire people with his personality. Izzy was a huge fan of Paul, and I found myself sitting and wondering if a similar fate awaited my brother.

"Where is he? Where is my boy?" screamed a voice from outside the room.

I knew who it was even before I saw her face. Nothing on GOD's green earth was going to keep her from seeing him and deep down, I believed that he liked it that way. I peeked out from the last room down the long corridor and saw the nurse pointing in my direction. I thought to myself that it would be in everybody's best interest to get this woman into his room before she tore the hospital a new wing. She absolutely loved Izzy with every ounce of her being and he knew this to be the case, but sometimes their love for each other caused them to butt heads.

Upon entering the room, she nearly collapsed. She has seen him hospitalized many times before, but never unconscious or non-responsive. She reached out to touch his chest, then bent forward to kiss his cheek. She then picked up the chart by his bedside and began asking questions:

"What happened?"

"He fell!"

"How did he fall?"

"He was walking toward the podium on the left side of the stage to speak to the kids, when all of a sudden, he tripped and banged his head."

"What did the doctors say?"

"Haven't got anything official as of yet. Nurses say he is stable."

She backed up and let all of her weight rest in the chair against the wall opposite Izzy's hospital bed. Drenched in her tears of fear, she began to reminisce about the times when she had sat in a similar room with Izzy.

"You know that boy was born an asthmatic, right? He would suffer with it repeatedly and every so often, we would find ourselves sitting in the emergency room having to have them administer some breathing solution to open up his lungs. I would be terrified for him, but we always made it

through. I know he is a fighter and it will take more than a bang on the head to stop his progression."

I nodded my head in agreement.

"I can remember when he tore away the skin from his left foot. Trying to follow behind Jixx, he was on the back of the bike and his foot got tangled in the spokes. At first, when he rolled his sock down to his ankle, there was pain and a bit of blood but he wouldn't give in because his didn't want to cry in front of the older boys. When he finally took the sock off later that evening, he had ripped the skin and tissue away so bad, that his skeletal bones were exposed."

Amazed at this new-found information, I sat quietly and sponged it all in.

"And of course, he wasn't able to walk for a while. I cannot tell you how many weekly trips to New York Hospital we made. He would be laid up thinking I was his personal servant - I knew he loved all the attention, too. I really didn't mind, though, because he is mine- but sometimes I'd want to spank his butt! Plus, I could tell when he was getting better because that humongous appetite reappeared."

"Oh and let me tell you about the infamous cheekbone incident! Well, this is where his hard head created a problem because he would not listen. He was told NOT to play basketball with the other kids in gym class because he could risk injury. He was the so-called star of his high school team and, as most teenagers do, he thought he would be exempt from the threat. As the official story goes, he went against what was advised and began playing a pickup game in class. He says someone threw a pass that he was going to intercept and out of the corner of his eye he saw this burly kid running in his direction. By the time he realized the kid couldn't stop, they had already collided and he bounced backwards and collided with the wall. We later found out that he had a hairline fracture to his cheekbone."

I sat motionless. My lower body was resisting the animation but my facial expressions were speaking volumes.

"Do you know this boy was trying to play again a few weeks later, even after the doctors told him that if the bone was hit and pushed out of place, they would have to cut him from his ear to his jaw and insert pins? Luckily, all of the boys in the neighborhood along with his coaches refused to allow him near the court. He came home complaining to me about how he was being ignored! "

"Ignored?" I said with a sarcastic smile.

"Um Hmm! I bet he didn't tell you about the time he fell on the concrete trying to impress the little girls by wearing those steel-over-the-shoe skates. He was trying to show off and be the center of attention. There he was skating up and down in front of my sister's apartment building in Brooklyn. He was stomping so hard that the sparks were shooting out from under his feet. Unfortunately for him, he didn't have on any padding and his super powers took the night off, so when his back wheel got tangled with another skater, he took flight. When he landed, it was chin to concrete and he slid about ten feet. His front tooth was ground in half as a result."

She went on and on about Izzy and the sometimes funny but always action-packed adventures he would create for her to partake in. Whether she wanted to or not, it seemed as if he kept her on alert and active in his young life and today is just another example of her allegiance to him.

Sinisterly, I responded with a tale of my own. I told her about the time when I went with Izzy and our coach to the hospital to obtain stitches to his forehead after getting caught with an elbow on the basketball court. He told me that he was going to get in and out quickly and we looked at him like he was crazy. Everyone knows that a visit to the Emergency Room is at least a five hour visit and we thought he might be a little delusional from the hit. He looked back at me with that face he makes - you know, the one with the raised right eyebrow. He told me that if we were not seen within 15 minutes of being there, he was going to *'get their attention'*. Coach and I paid no attention to the comment as we walked through the sliding door to the hospital. Once we visited the registration area and were told to sit down until his name was called, I noticed Izzy looking at the clock with an irritated demeanor. Sixteen minutes later, he rose up, stumbled his way to the middle of the waiting area and laid down in the middle of the floor. All of the nurses and hospital employees went into panic mode, screaming, "Get him up! Get him up!" They rushed over to attend to Izzy and take him back to be worked on. We sat there in amazement as they picked him up, placed him in a rolling bed and wheeled him into a room. Before they disappeared behind the door, I saw Izzy's face and he had that eyebrow raised.

Izzy's mom got up from her seat before I could finish my story and cracked a grin from the left side of her face. She closed her eyes and began shaking her head from East to West. I don't know if she really heard what I was saying, or if she was succumbing to the pressures. For a few moments at least, I was able to keep the chuckles going to offset the true pain and anxiety that I know was permeating her being. I wondered what she was truly thinking at that moment and if she was silently making amends with him of any ill-will that was currently lingering between them. Izzy had become exceptional at holding grudges and dismembering a relationship whenever he felt threatened or devalued. Rarely would he ever communicate this to anyone. He was not one who wore his emotions on his sleeve. He was ferociously guarded and lacked the will to become vulnerable. Instead, he internalized his feelings, conjured up the worst pain imaginable and attached it to the targeted subject. Then, unbeknownst to the other person, used that pairing is ultimately to justify cutting him or her out of his life. It was a unique skill to have, actually, and I could see how earlier in his life, developing a way to disconnect from an unfit reality would have helped him survive, but as you mature and progress through life, it could be a catalyst for introversion and a hindrance to building relationships.

I left the room to give them some time alone. I always believed that it was much easier to emotionally disrobe when you were alone than with an audience, and I knew that this was a perfect time to take a walk. I began strolling down the brightly-lit hallway, passing by room after room of the sick, the elderly and the wounded. I knew we were at the best place for Izzy to get help, but I felt as if I was continuously peering through death's big bay window.

I continued to walk along the white-tiled floor and dodge in and out of the sea of nurses and doctors, who were somehow providing healthcare services on a smile-and-run basis. With my head held low, I began to focus on the black speckles that were fused within the surface of the tile. My mid-tempo strides, coupled with an elongated stare, put me in somewhat of a zombified state of hypnosis. Locked within a repetitive pattern of freckled white squares with dividing black lines, I reconnected with one of our childhood pastimes. *Step on a crack and break your mother's back* was a game we all played and without hesitation, I began trying to place my footsteps within the square and not step on the black lines that divided them. In a weird way, I was paying homage to my very best friend by taking a walk on the *"tiled"* side.

CHAPTER 9:
THE FIVE HOUR BUS RIDE

"HEY, GUYS! YOU CAN EITHER MOVE OR BE REMOVED!"

As we walked through the sliding glass doors of the bus station, we overheard a police officer speaking to a group of homeless folks who were bundled up in old sleeping bags and dusty quilts. It didn't bother us too much, because it wasn't the first time we would encounter people on the street and we figured it wouldn't be the last. Izzy garnered his double-strapped knapsack filled with traveling snacks and Spiderman comic books. Around his neck was a thin, white string which was just long enough to allow the 5-inch squared red and white cardboard sign to rest on his chest. On the sign was a letter that corresponded to the community group and the allotted bus route that would take him five hours north of New York City.

"See, there is the big, grey dog I told you about!"

"Yeah, that is cool. Looks like those dogs at the racetrack your uncle takes us to on Long Island."

"Yeah, I think the same people own this, too. You know they got a lot of dough. My uncle and his friends always leave there talking about how the dog is not to be trusted."

"Race you to the end?"

"Bet!"

Izzy took off running. I was beginning to make up ground until he yelled out,

"Step on the crack and break your mother's back!"

We both immediately became aware of the alignment within the floor patters and began to take our following steps with great care. Izzy's mom was walking behind us, wheeling her son's large, black suitcase.

"Stop running, guys! C'mon, this way, we gotta check in."

We took a left turn then walked up an incline. We came to a group of people that were hovered around three or four wooden tables and searched for Izzy's name. To our right was a group of kids who remembered Izzy from his previous trips and we were all filled to the rim with excitement and anticipation.

"I can't wait to get going! Where are you gonna sit?" asked one of the kids.

"I don't know; as long as I am not near the bathroom, I'm cool," said Izzy.

The same kid turned to me and asked, "What about you?"

At that very moment, it hit me across the face that I wasn't getting

on the bus. My travel seat was going to be underground, on the subway, in-

between Izzy's mom and a total stranger. My once sky-high level of

excitement took a nose dive, hit rock bottom and then exploded into

fragments of despair. I could feel the lukewarm water rising from behind

my eyes, instantly swelling my tear ducts and accompanied by a lonesome

feeling that engulfed my heart. I had forgotten that this *"Au Revoir"* was for

Izzy and Izzy only. I was there to wish him farewell and give him a friendly

B-12 shot in the arm. Izzy's mom had known that it was always an

emotional departure for each of them, and having me present might help

Izzy go without shedding a room full of tears; she knew he was prideful of

his manly image and would be very reluctant to cry in front of me. Life in

the hood had groomed us to be tough and stand firm in the face of

adversity and we played our positions without fail.

Izzy looked at us through his window seat in the middle of the bus.

He pressed his forehead firmly up against the glass and waved goodbye. His

heavy breathing caused the window to slightly fog beneath his lips. He was

mouthing something, but I was unable to decipher the words. I looked over

at his mom as she waved him farewell and wiped the streaming tears from

her face. Izzy deliberately fogged up a section on the window and used his

pointer finger to draw an eye, then a heart and a letter "u". The big gray dog-bus carrying such precious cargo pulled away from its parked space, made a left turn and then slowly disappeared outside of the darkened tunnel. I stood there motionless and emotion-full, watching in complete awe as the leftover trail of black carbon smoke rose from atop the hot asphalt and blocked our vision - much like the closing of the final curtain on your favorite movie.

We made our way back through the bus depot, stepping over and dodging through the layers of homeless folks, down the wide, steel stairwell and into the subway station. I was silently thinking about the fun Izzy was having on the big grey bus and I was quite envious. On the crowded subway car, I took a seat in-between two large grownups and Izzy's mom stood in front clinging tightly to the metal pole that passengers use to keep them from falling while the train is in motion. I noticed that her left hand was resting on the small of her back as she bent forward slightly and wore a gentle grimace upon her face. I chuckled underneath my breath a bit as it became quite clear who the winner of our competition was. It was evident that somewhere along the line, Izzy must have taken a miss-step and placed his foot upon a crack in the floor.

Back home I sat on the sofa and watched the hands of the clock slap each other a high five on four different occasions. From what Izzy had described to me from his previous visits, I could envision the bus pulling into the town of Corning, NY and heading towards the high school. His new family would be waiting patiently with the other hosts as the bus would come to a halt and spit out each alien visitor one by one. The verification process of obtaining the right kid would take place much like an airline passenger verifying their respective parcels of luggage. He would walk into a sea of hugs and kisses and then be whisked away for a quick bite to relieve him from his five hour fast. It is during this time that he must start the process to release himself from his cocooned New York state of mind. He must begin to shed the blanketing survival mentality of *"ME"* and open himself up to the vulnerable conditions of *"WE"*.

During their car ride home, he would listen to all the wonderful things they had planned for his time there. Museum visits, swimming, tubing, family outings to the beach, picnics atop the waterfalls at Watkins Glen, playing his beloved basketball with the neighboring children and visits to Grandma and Grandpa Nessle's to climb his favorite tree and eat his favorite dish cooked especially for him- Rigatoni's with fresh homemade marinara sauce comprised of the tomatoes he would personally hand pick from their garden. He and his summertime sister would climb onto the back wall of the yard and watch as the Fourth of July fireworks illuminated their star-studded midnight sky.

Frolicking alongside the birds and the bees on the wide open farmlands, and feeling the prickly sensations of the green blades of grass massaging your bare feet, is a long way away from the confines of the city's light gray concrete flooring and seas of graffiti-laden brick buildings. Whenever any living organism is thrust into a new environment in which it must survive, it begins to develop certain characteristics to do so. We have witnessed subtle adaptations within the animal kingdom like changing of diets, the growth of extra limbs not seen on the original species, and the ability to live amongst the intruding human population. In Izzy's case, he learned to trim what was unnecessary from his street-life personality and create a revised version of himself.

Over the years of repetitive Summer visits and maneuvering between two completely different worlds, Izzy had become masterful at managing his two different personas. He was a simple kid living a complex life under difficult circumstances, but somehow, he kept his skeletons in the back of the closets. During his summertime visits, he was in a world that shielded him from the threats of random gunfire, armed robbery and spontaneous domestic violence. There, he could be a normal kid, whose enormous imagination had a chance to be nurtured and grow wings. What became evident to Izzy out there was the fact that there was more to this game of life than just making it out from his current lifestyle. What he believed was that he had been granted temporary access into a world that exists only on screen. He realized that he wasn't going to find any lookalikes or body doubles in that neighborhood and he was well aware that all eyes were on him like a science project.

I looked up at the clock again and realized that it was getting late. The lights on the basketball court would be illuminating soon and the die-hard neighborhood basketball population would arise from their darkened coffins of rest. Bouncing balls, loud boastful talk and real tough competition was the norm amongst these creatures of the night and into the midnight hour, you would hear the roar of the crowds. This was the place where our dreams would come alive. This was the exit wound from the land of broken promises and stifled momentum. This was where Izzy and I spent the majority of our time looking up into the stars and hoping for a miracle - but I knew this outing would be different. Something would be wrong. Maybe the round orange and black balls would be square, the lights would not shine as bright, or the demeanor of the crowd would be toxic. Somehow, deep down in my gut, I felt that tonight should be filled with VHS movies and Jiffy Pop popcorn. After settling in and pressing play on the machine, I returned to my seat only to hear a crunching sound coming from under the television set. I jumped up and hit the stop button on the VHS recorder. When I removed the black rectangle casing from the slot, it was closely followed by the spillage of all its insides. I sat back onto the couch with my legs feeling too heavy to move and thought to myself that without Izzy, this Summer was going to be rough.

CHAPTER 10:
A COMPLEX TRUTH

I started my trek back towards the area of the hospital that Izzy was in. The worried look on my face must have been tale-telling, based on all of the well wishes I received from passing staff members. While rounding the final corner, I noticed a rush of people in white overcoats dashing towards the room. I hurried my pace and upon entering the room, witnessed an overanxious crowd hovering over his bed as if performing a surgical procedure.

"What is going on?" I asked.

No one responded. I began moving my feet towards the bed, parting the crowd with the ferocity of an over-protective parent.

I began to shout, *"Why are y'all covering him like that? What's wrong with him?"*

"He flat-lined," replied one of the nurses.

"Flat-lined? What do you mean he flat-lined?"

"Sir, please stand back! We need you to move away from the patient."

The medical staff were operating in a frenzy! Chaos had burst into the room and begun throwing its weight around. Three male doctors ushered me out and into a waiting area, where I saw Izzy's mom crying with a heavy heart.

"He's not gonna make it - I can feel it."

I didn't want to entertain that thought at all, so I reached way down and pulled *Mr. Positive* out of my back pocket and replied,

"Sure he'll make it. Don't even think like that. He is far from seeing the other side – plus, we've got too many things left to accomplish. GOD is not calling him yet. This is just a momentary pit stop along our long journey."

She grabbed me and bear-hugged me as if I was GOD himself. Immediately, I was able to feel all of the bottled-up pain she had been holding up to this point. It was a numbing and humbling experience and at that moment, an urge was bestowed upon me and I felt the need to call her *"ma"*.

"Ma, don't shatter your faith. You know that's a strong individual in there."

We both sat down in the waiting area with our heads bent and silently searching for answers. I had never prayed so much and so hard for one particular thing to occur - and I knew that if GOD was listening, he probably had rolled his eyes a few times from being annoyed with all of our repetitious calls.

Patiently we waited.

...and waited.

...and waited.

...and waited some more.

Finally, we were greeted by the doctor in charge of Izzy's care.

"We are extremely pleased to tell you that the patient has responded to our efforts and has been placed on twenty-four hour surveillance so that we can closely monitor his progress. I suggest you folks go home and get some rest. Visiting hours are from nine-thirty to five-thirty tomorrow."

"Thanks, Doctor! We appreciate all your help".

We gathered our senses and our belongings and headed for the hospital exit. Once outside the air-conditioned safe-haven, the humidity attacked our persons like determined paparazzi. I tugged at my light blue, dry-fit shirt, pinching both sides of my collar between my pointer and thumb fingers, to allow air to circulate my body. I tilted my head backwards to give thanks to the man above and noticed how bright GOD's hallway lights were. The vast midnight sky did not stand a chance against the glow of HIS spherical spotlight and its illustrious background singers. I paused for a moment to quietly exhale all the fear and anxieties that had been kind enough to accompany me all day, and felt an overwhelming feeling of comfort being bestowed upon me.

Later that night, after a couple of Yoga stretches and devouring a cup of herbal green tea, I heard the phone ring. I hesitated to move towards the sound of the ringing object, as I was a bit afraid of what information might be revealed to me. The caller ID flashed the ten-digit number of the hospital and on the fifth chime, I got the nerve to pick up the receiver.

"Hello?"

"Hey" replied the crackled voice on the other end of the line.

"Izzy?"

"Yeah."

"Thank GOD! How are you feeling?"

"I'm ok. A lil' sore from all those people punching on my chest and I got a slight headache, but other than that, I think I'm fine."

I felt my eyes begin to swell from the inner pool of joy that was rising feverishly and preparing to break a levy. The heavy burden of an unknown future without my best friend was suddenly discarded once I heard his raspy, sedated voice through the receiver.

"I'll be right there!"

"No. Wait until tomorrow. I'll see you when you get here and please don't alert anyone yet."

I found it to be an extremely odd request that his return to consciousness be kept in secrecy. As I hung up the phone, my instincts were to call everyone who would care that he was functional again, but I had made a promise. I rolled back the sheets and laid down for the night. Two quick hand claps and the room became dark, but my adrenaline was operating at full-tilt, with no signs of tapering off. My mind began racing in all different directions. Had he learned some staggering news that he must prepare us for? We have so much to do and so little time in which to do it! Our purpose had always been to set the most outrageous goals, overcome our fears of success and failures, then take over the world. I knew my position still remained the same, but something about Izzy's phone call didn't seem right. Could it be that I was just a little paranoid or suffering

from a slight case of emotional fatigue? I continued to hold my perfect

parallel position, turning my back towards the floor and focusing in on the

circular motions of the dusty ceiling fan above me, until my brain began

waiving the checkered flag signaling the end of this exhausting mental race.

I began to hear a familiar ripping sound of rubber tires continuously

crossing a metal grate. I felt the wind blow across my face and neck and

from below, came the stench of polluted water. From behind, I could feel

the shadowing presence of the four gigantic red-and-grey columns that had

always played the background during my times of revelation. I was again

standing in our most famous spot for dreaming: the middle of the

Queensboro Bridge, with both hands resting on the black steel railing and

eyes focused over the South Street Seaport and onto the twin towers of the

World Trade Center. Here is where Izzy and I would dream that one day we

would both own this monstrosity that stood head and shoulders above the

rest and seemingly had the audacity to poke at GOD's illustrious white

clouds with its glowing red antenna. Two towers, two friends. The process

of each owning one was as complex as figuring out the combination to a

Rubik's Cube with a fifth side, but the end result always felt right.

"I think I will take the antenna off the roof, because it looks as if it's

wearing one of those hats with the propeller. That's not fly."

"Yeah, it does. But I would just leave it the way it is. Whatever is occurring in those buildings is generating a lot of dough and when something ain't broke, don't fix it. I want the one with the best view of the Statue of Liberty and Brooklyn, so I can always look at my grandma's house to see how she is doing."

"You can just move her in there!"

"Nah, my grandpa's is not going for all of those people running through his living room. He would have a conniption! You know he doesn't play."

"True! I remember he gave me the look of the dead-eyed scorpion when we were last there to visit and I accidently tracked mud on his rug."

"Yeah, that's my dude. I gotta make it big because I promised him I would make something of myself. He listens to me and dares me to be great - always has, and I bet he always will. He is the one who named me."

"Word?"

"Yep. He said my name means warrior and signals strength. He always makes me feel good whenever we talk. Although, I did overhear him telling my mom that I had a lot of rage built up inside of me recently. He said that I had to find a way to channel it because if it spills out then I may unconsciously do something that I would regret. He fears that I may harm someone or even create a situation that may harm me."

"Whoa. That's deep. Did you ever tell him about what the Tall Man did to you?"

"No and I cannot ever let anyone know. There is way too much riding on that. You are the only one I told, so keep your mouth shut."

"Alright, I won't say a word. I just think it's awful."

"Hey, if I tell you something you must promise me to never tell a soul."

My heart skipped a beat. "Okay, I promise."

"Well, recently, the rage almost got out"

"What do you mean?"

"A few weeks ago I had to deal with an impromptu afternoon visit from Uncle Al and I decided to leave the house before all the madness started. Unfortunately, while walking through the front door of my building, I ran into Harland and he began his usual bullying tactics and slapping me around. At that moment it seemed pointless to fight or even to show any emotion. I just remained silent and took every bit of the harassment. I felt the fear leave my body only to be replaced with an immeasurable amount of anger. After he let me go, that forceful rage led me to gather a few items and pace myself for vengeance.

I walked up onto the steps of the community center, through the double doors and into the games room. A force directed me to lift four marble pool balls and put them into my pocket. From there, I was directed to the dollar store and bought a black wool ski mask. I also needed something that would hold the balls in place and I couldn't go home to get what I needed, so I went to the Laundromat on the corner and grabbed a pillow case from someone's load of clothes. I waited until it got dark, then I walked across the roof, unscrewed the light bulb and sat in the pitch black stairwell waiting for Harland to come home. I had put my mask on to cover my face and the pillow case had the four pool balls housed close together with the use of four rubber bands. Dressed in all black, I took on the persona of a shadow as I waited for about three hours. I had every intention of bashing him in the head repeatedly until the rage was gone. As I sat in that stairwell, I felt a tug at my shirt and voices in my ears telling me how disappointed they were and how they didn't want to have anything further to do with me. It was the voices of my Fresh Air Fund family and my grandparents. I didn't want to disappoint them in any way, so I got up from *my hiding place and went home. That evening, those voices saved TWO*

lives."

With my eyes still focused on the towers, I dropped my jaw and my heart sank a few notches below my knees. I always knew my best friend was dealing with issues unbefitting a young teenager, but the level to which it had grown was a real cause for concern. The secret he made me swear to could have made me an accomplice to a crime. I couldn't help but think of his grandfather's words of wisdom. The chilling story that just spilled from his lips and the way he didn't blink an eye when telling it made me question to myself whether there were two people living behind those hospitable brown eyes, or he was losing his grip on reality. I knew Harland wasn't the true cause of his pain, he just exacerbated it. We didn't dwell on the secret for long, as the dwindling sun rays suddenly became shy and hid behind the world-famous Manhattan skyline. With the wind picking up and the cool air shooting through the air pockets of the bridge, we decided to gather our heads from the top of the Trade Center and journey back down to our desolate slice of life.

CHAPTER 11:
PERSPECTIVE

On my way to the hospital, my mind could not stop the continuous anticipation of the worst. As we all do in the presence of the unknown, the only thought I could conjure up was that of complete ruin. My heart did more than skip a few beats... It played a song - a violent rap song with a contagious looped beat and no chorus. The pulsating blood flow that ravaged my veins and arteries was on a mission to keep my heart pumping at a feverish pace and challenge the notion that my deodorant was indeed heat-activated.

I entered the sliding glass door of the building, filled with jumbled emotions and a nervous demeanor. I walked down the illuminated hallway and stood tall amongst the gathering crowd, waiting to board the elevator and make the trek skyward. Fear leapt from my back and pressed the button to summon the elevator, and together we stepped into the tightly-spaced enclosure. Seven stops later, when I emerged from the squared contraption, I was dripping with anxiety and partially paralyzed by the seemingly non-stop propaganda I had been feeding myself. I knew I had to gather my wits and steer my ship straight before I entered Izzy's room; I didn't want to create more of a stir in the air than what was already looming. I tightened my belt buckle and shook myself clear of my mental anguish, before opening the heavy wooden door and walking into the room, where I saw Izzy sitting quietly in a chair, gazing out of a window.

"Do you know the REAL difference between a bird and an ant?" he asks.

"No. You tell me."

"PERSPECTIVE! Far too often we engulf ourselves with the tedious occurrences and insignificant events that develop on a daily basis and we forget that it's all part of a bigger picture. The beauty that is all around us for our enjoyment and satisfaction gets overshadowed by our inability to raise our heads and look past our feet. Do you know what I mean?"

"I believe I do, but at this very moment, I am just happy to see you functioning again."

Izzy turned to face me and grinned a half-hearted thank you.

"How are you, my friend? Are you in pain? Can you walk? Do you remember any of what happened?" I asked.

"My memory of the incident is a little vague, but I believe my previous thought patterns gave way to the actions that caused my brief demise."

"What do you mean?"

"For so long I have been dangling myself between two worlds - One which held my true reality and one which garnered a distinct possibility. I have maneuvered through these worlds since the days of my childhood and the door through which I would pass began splintering some years ago. As I began to grow older, my voice of reality began to make it more and more difficult to turn the knob and walk into my desired land of possibilities. It made me fearful, lonely and filled with despair. When GOD decided to take my grandparents a few years ago, it left a big hole in my structural foundation. I began thinking about how great it would be to sit and talk with them again. Irrational thoughts began to take control and soon, those thoughts started to become actions. "

"Actions? What do you MEAN by actions?"

"Well, for starters, do you remember the scratches on the passenger side of my vehicle?"

"Yes," I replied.

"Well, they didn't happen while the car was parked. No one mysteriously swiped my car and caused those awful imperfections. It was I. I was the perpetrator. It happened as I was on my way home and began to feel this deep depressive feeling come over me. It saddened me to the point of shedding a cupful of tears. I felt as helpless and as insignificant as I had

when I was a little kid stuck under the bed trying to escape the pain and anxiety of a world torn apart by alcohol and drugs. Violence had stripped me of my innocence and I always wondered when it would return to finish me off. I wanted to end the chase - plus my legs were tired from running from what I felt to be the inevitable. So, I pulled the wheel quickly to the right and when I hit the guardrail it jolted me back to my senses. Luckily, there were no witnesses to the incident and I went home."

"WHAT! ARE YOU SERIOUS? WHAT WERE YOU THINKING?" I yelled at him, flabbergasted.

"Hence part of the problem I have. I wasn't thinking. I was feeling. I felt it was all a dream until I was jolted back to the reality of what I was doing. I mean, I had thought about that action many times before, but I never intended to act on it. On my good days, I will tell you that I have too much to lose, but on those certain occasions when the wind blows left instead of right and rain falls without any visible clouds, the answer I spew may shock you."

"Dude, I think we need to go seek help!"

"Help? What truly is help? Sitting down on someone's couch, revealing my innermost thoughts, insecurities and vulnerabilities to a complete stranger, only to have them reach over and hit the timer and tell me my hour is up; how about making myself transparent to someone who thinks they know me so they can now pass judgment on me going forward and perhaps leak my most cherished secrets the second they get angry with me. Nah, been there and done that and it kind of makes me feel even worse. I have witnessed that scenario played out too many times and all the patient, to the 'help', is a faceless vehicle to boost their income. I am nobody's fool. I don't want to be a topic for discussion over someone's dinner table. My life is what it is and the direct result of the choices I have made - so I have to be the one to suit up and deal with it."

"But together we can tag team it. We can beat those demons and find a way to minimize those hopeless thoughts and illicit feelings."

"My friend, I confide in you because of your loyalty and our long history together. Unfortunately, this is a math equation that I must find the answer to alone. Before this accident occurred, I was looking out into the sea of kids and I found my young self in the crowd. I looked directly into the eyes of the young me and whispered a directive to be more than anyone expected and to never bow out. I became emotional, because I could now see on the outside what I had been sheltering on the inside for all those years. At that point, as a young kid, I had already made an attempt on my life once already and the fighter in me was pissed. I wanted to kill off the side of me that felt scared and afraid, but I couldn't do so without injuring the conquistador on the other side. I have always been a conflicted soul, and my new reality is that I can't dissipate either."

"So what happens now?" I asked.

Izzy turned to look over his shoulder and back out of the window. He seemed to be searching for a definitive answer to an elusive question. His vast mental rolodex of solutions had encountered an empty slot, which to him was highly irregular and extremely unorthodox. He took a deep breath and exhaled the word that we began this conversation with:

PERSPECTIVE.

He climbed back into bed and pulled the covers up towards his chin. I didn't know what to think as I sat there silently, not knowing whether I would soon be scheduling another speaking engagement, or planning a funeral. As a child, he once told me that he didn't expect to live past the age of twenty-five. I never really paid any attention to those comments, but I could now see the results of a life without any true expectations. He talked about perspective, but I don't think he saw his value to me, to his family and to those who had benefitted from his genuine love for others outside of his invisible fence. I believe his perspective was derived only from what he had encountered in the past and not what was awaiting him in the future.

My dilemma had now become two-fold. First, I had to continue to build on the trust we had in each other and keep him comfortable enough to share what was going on inside that complex brain maze of his and secondly, I needed to make him aware of the God-given gifts that he had been blessed with and how not maximizing those gifts created a rift in the natural order of sowing seeds and reaping rewards. The way I saw it, this man had been blessed with natural talents and abilities, which made those who cross paths with him feel more valued afterwards than before they met. He had a heart as big as the Grand Canyon and if he was not supposed to do something with it, then he wouldn't have made it this far, given his highly tumultuous past and upbringing.

Yes, it is just like he said.

PERSPECTIVE.

For the next thirty minutes, we wallowed in an awkward silence that neither party knew how to crawl out from. I had much to discuss with him and many questions I needed answered. We watched the programs which were regulated by the hospital staff and chuckled at a few of the blunders on the sports center highlight reel. I knew it had taken a lot of courage to set aside his enormous amount of pride and share that piece of information with me. Although I knew the conversation needed to resume at some point, I didn't want to beat it to death by badgering the witness. He knew that I wouldn't just sweep this under the rug. I wondered if by telling me in this manner, it would force him to be cognizant and accountable for his thoughts and actions going forward. Maybe it was too overwhelming for his pride to just ask for help and by releasing that piece of information in a way which would not be considered as weak, he was able to verbally extend his arms and point his palms towards the sky without shrieking a victim-like cry.

I tried to ease the moment and break through the thick wall of silence by changing the subject altogether and I knew just the six words to remedy the situation:

"Think the Knicks got a chance?"

CHAPTER 12:
FLOWERS IN THE GARDEN

In the 1980's, we were sure hoping for a miracle to happen on 34th street. Our beloved New York Knickerbockers were all but a division two college team – with the exception of the *King* of New York – *Bernard King*. When Patrick Ewing was acquired in the draft in '85, we thought Santa had brought us an early gift in June and the bright lights of the Big Apple illuminated as if the ball was being dropped and it was the start of a new year.

New Yorkers were giddy with the possibility of winning multiple NBA championships for years to come, and our five-man crew fell right in line. The inhabitants of the Big Apple desperately wanted to wear the orange and blue uniforms to show support for our heroes, who would lead us from the dungeons of despair to hoisting the Larry O'Brien trophy. On the sidelines, we had one of the best coaches in Hubie Brown and on paper, a would-be dynamic duo in King and Ewing. We all purchased brand-new replica jerseys with the familiar bold Knicks logo on the chest area, but when it came to whose name would be on the back, well, to say the least, it was a challenge.

Izzy and I played guard positions, but Izzy refused to wear Rory Sparrow's number two. Instead, he donned Patrick Ewing's number thirty-three. He thought Rory Sparrow was the weakest point guard in the league and swore up and down that he was better than him - that was, until Rory showed up to a basketball camp we attended and stole the ball from Izzy three times in a row.

Gustavo, aka School Bus Gus, wore Bernard King's number thirty. He was the elder statesman of the group by two whole years and the one with the wickedest mouth. He was of Jamaican decent and stood about five foot, nine inches tall, but relentlessly insisted that he was six feet. He always had a sheepish grin on his face and always smelled as if he just finished cooking with a lot of curry powder and onions. The nick-name of 'School bus' was given to him because he was only interested in girls younger than he. He would always keep gum and candy in his right pocket as '*ice breakers*' or '*gifts*' for the young ladies. We called it '*bait*'.

David, aka Dancing Davey, was forced to wear Louis Orr's number fifty-five. He was a tall, slim, Hispanic, six foot, four inch break dancer originally from the Bronx. We realized that he suffered from "*stand still – itis*". If we were standing in a group having a conversation, Davey would be moving and pop locking as if he was in a dance battle. I always noticed the looks we got from folks who found it funny to see our group standing at ease and one in perpetual motion. Gustavo always said that the Knicks's small forward, Louis Orr, was everything except a basketball player. He also thought the same about Davey. So after all the dust had settled and the last time out had been called, Davey emerged from our huddle with the double-nickel number on his jersey and a "**DNP**" next to his name.

And finally there's Calvin, aka Copy Cat Cal. Calvin was our Caucasian ideas man. Unfortunately for us, the ideas were always secondary. Nothing was ever original. His gems were always a derivative of something that had already been done. Triple C, which is what he became known as, was infamous for claiming a theft of an idea he was working on and always letting us know that he was one day closer to dreaming and achieving his masterpiece. Izzy urged him to wear number 0. No one on the Knicks team wore the number and when asked why he chose 0, Izzy responded *"...there is no one like Calvin anywhere!"*

Going to a game at Madison Square Garden was like heaven for us. We would make sure our uniforms were pressed before we left the house. Our walk to the subway station was our time to talk strategy against tonight's opponent, then hop the turnstile and onto the platform and wait for our iron chariot. Once we entered into the stadium, we would rush into the restrooms to make sure our attire resembled that of our heroes, before attempting to sneak down into the lower levels, carrying the wild idea that we could sit on the Knicks' bench and nobody would notice. Each time we'd try, we would get close enough to see the steam ejecting from the heads of the players, but get turned away by the same usher who would always thwart our plans. School Bus Gus used to always blame Davey because of his inability to walk in a straight line without wiggling.

"Look Davey, you gotta either stay in your seat or walk like a regular human. Here we are, trying to blend in with the team, and you got hands and feet flying like a bungee jumper."

"Leave him alone, Gus," warned Cal. *"You never know, when I start my league, the NBPA (National Ball Players Association), Davey is going to be the lead choreographer for all the team dancers."*

The three of us looked at each other and rolled our eyes.

"NBPA?" said Izzy. *"That's not gonna work. Who's gonna own your teams...crack heads and winos?*

"See, this is the problem with you dudes - you don't have any vision."

"Well, I've got vision," chimed Gus, *"and so do the other eighteen-thousand people in here who can see this fool gyrating like a broken slinky!"*

After a few chuckles, we would all slap high fives with each other, commemorating our feeble attempt at becoming official Knickerbockers for the day, then it was back to our seats for the remainder of the game.

About two and a half hours later, we would emerge from the undertow of Madison Square Garden angry, agitated and always fighting over who was to blame for the loss. I always wondered how four quarters of play at twelve minutes each added up to one hundred and fifty minutes of '*time*'. The way the public school system taught me to compute numbers, I always came up with forty eight minutes of play. Even if you factored in thirty minutes for the half-time festivities, you should only have been at seventy-eight minutes. That still left seventy-two minutes unaccounted for, but I guess that was part of the mystique surrounding Madison Square Garden. Once the night air had a chance to caress our faces and we noticed the white smoke streaking upward from the Manhattan manhole covers, I knew that it was the ringing of the bell which would signal the start of our heated discussions:

"If Darryl Walker could hit a dang fifteen-foot jump shot, he probably would be considered a legit player," came the complaint from School Bus Gus.

"Don't just blame D-W! At least he plays defense. Rory can't guard ANYBODY! Every guard in the league probably looks at the schedule in the beginning of the year and circles the Knicks dates ,then sends flowers and a limo to pick him up to make sure he is at the game on time so they can have a career night," Izzy piped up.

"Yep! And did you see little Louie sitting on the bench dancing and laughing? I told you he and Davey boy was related. He would probably serve the Knicks better if he was working the concession stand selling two-dollar franks. I know Bernard be looking at Hubie like: dude, we need help!"

"Hahahahaha! We could probably give the Knicks a run for the money. I know we couldn't be any worse."

And on and on the drudging would go. The knickerbockers were our beloved team and as native New Yorkers, we felt as if they were our extended family and it was our birth right to be able to criticize and ridicule them, but should an outsider attempt to do so, we would fight like gladiators to defend them.

Izzy was always the implied leader of our group - not because he was the biggest or the baddest, but because he took the time to render us all important. He knew when to step back from the limelight and let each of us enjoy our time to shine. On the way home from our adventures , he created a ritual of beat-boxing with his mouth and hands; banging on anything that would make a sound, so that Davey could do his dance routines and people would stop and admire. I knew it gave Davey a huge sense of pride and a stronger belief in himself, because you could see Davey begin to stand up taller and wiggle a lot harder.

I always believed that Izzy got satisfaction from pumping people up and watching them unravel from their own prisonous cocoon; it seemed to please him in a way that nothing else would. When confronted about what he was up to, he would laugh it off as if he was making a joke, but the results were undeniable. He was absolutely doing the most, but behind the scenes, he was benefiting the least. Deep down, I believed that he needed a return on his emotional investments, but he relentlessly refused to allow himself to be vulnerable enough for us to do so. I knew my best buddy was suffering with a loaded heart, feeling like there was nowhere to turn and no one who could truly understand his pain. I felt his discomfort for years and this led us to become less like neighborhood friends and more like twin brothers. Whether he believed it or not, I wouldn't ever abandon nor belittle our godly connection.

The mask which one wears to camouflage pain and despair can be altered to reflect all sorts of non-truths, but the heart and eyes of a person beat and blink to a different rhythm. The irrepressible disappointments and continued mental anguish they experience are slightly visible to the everyday observer and I've come to realize that their actions are usually counterintuitive to their innermost feelings.

On the train ride home, I always focused in on the faces and body language of our subway-car mates. I would always think to myself that the diversity on the train was a microcosm of the world we lived in. People of all races, creeds and color tolerating each other within close quarters for a short period of time, only to get what they wanted, but as soon as the goal was obtained and the escape hatch released, they'd flee the scene and forget their interactions like roaches when the lights were turned on.

Time waits for no one and we were closing in on our nightly curfew as we made our journey back across the Hudson River. With only a few scheduled train stops away from our destination, we encountered an electrical dead spot and momentarily, the lights went out. Our car came to a halt in the dark tunnel and everyone became crippled with silence. A few short minutes passed, then suddenly, the lights flickered before resuming their original state of illumination. Without a warning, the door to the connecting car slid open. Appearing from the shadowy walkway, entered a dark-skinned man wearing a brown leather jacket and wool skull cap. He stepped through, then forcefully slid the connecting car door shut with a bang. He looked to his left, then scanned the car until his ears were perpendicular to his shoulders. He stood about three feet from where we were sitting and when he saw us, he raised his arms and made a shooting noise from the makeshift gun he created with his hands and fingers. We all were jolted back in shock as we watched this *"knock off"* gunslinger blow the invisible smoke away from the barrel of his fingertips, then flip them backwards and into the pocket holster of his unevenly cut-off shorts. Once our unmasked marauder had moved on down the prairie to win yet another gun fight, Gus jumped out of his seat and said to the crowd:

"I'm so sorry y'all had to witness that!"

With his hands gliding through the air as if he was on stage presenting something, he went on to say:

"My brothers and I want to offer our sincerest apologies because had it not been for our rush to get to Madison Square Garden and support the Knicks tonight, this would never have happened. You have just witnessed what happens when our daddy doesn't take his medication! "

All the passengers onboard that subway car chuckled as if they were at a comedy show and engaged in conversations until we reached our stop. When the doors opened, we exited the car to the roar of an enormous applause, which stayed with us all the way home.

CHAPTER 13:
BACK TO NEVER-NEVER LAND

Some weeks later, Izzy received a letter from someone he had not heard from in over twenty years. He seemed awkwardly surprised when he dislodged the glue from in-between the overlapping flap and pocket-like portion of the envelope. He removed an egg-shell colored piece of stationery, which held the insignia of **M. Rozan M.D.** From the look on Izzy's face, I took it that this letter was a good thing - and good news always trumps bad news, especially when you already struggle for positive mental space within the framework of big-city blues.

"Well, don't just stand there! What does it say?"

"Wow! It's an invitation for a reunion!" he replied.

"A reunion? "

"Yeah. It seems like my old Fresh Air Fund friends are getting together. It's been such a long time since I have seen any of them. What if they don't remember me?"

"Remember you? Let's think about this for a moment. Some twenty-plus years ago, an ethnic little boy leaves his urban neighborhood every summer and travels hundreds of miles away to reside in a Caucasian-dominant suburb, where the children there had probably never encountered

someone from another race. Oh, I will bet money that you were not only the talk of the town, but unforgettably etched in their minds forever!"

We both took a time out and chuckled simultaneously at that vividly-painted picture.

"So, what do you think? Should I go?"

"Of course you should go. It will be great to change your scenery for a while and reminisce with friends from a joyous time in your life. Also, you never know who will be called home - as we agree that tomorrow is not promised to anyone."

"True; I can definitely attest to that! Will you come with me?

I squished my face up as if I were tasting lemons.

"You want me to go with you? I know they don't want to see me, plus I will be out of place as I don't have any memories to fall back on - and I won't know anyone."

"You know me! And that's all it will take. I'd really appreciate, bud."

"Ok. Give me the who, the what and the where...."

Izzy really didn't have to twist my arm. At last, here was a chance to visit *Never-Never Land* and I wasn't about to miss it, nor was I going to let him know how curious I was about his *"other"* set of friends. All the summers that Izzy spent away and all the adventures I would hear of when he would return home were things I knew nothing of, but was silently intrigued because of the joy it brought to him. They say you can't miss what you never had, but in an odd way, I felt as if I *HAD* already met those folks and lived through those adventures via the vivid recollection of their narrator.

Izzy dialed the number printed on the stationery, attempting to RSVP to the event. Through the speaker of his cell phone, I could hear a woman's voice respond to his initial greeting of *"hello"*. Once he identified himself to the woman holding the other end of the wireless connection, the audible return was that of a loud scream. As the conversation progressed, I noticed a change in the demeanor and body language of my best buddy. I assumed that he recognized the woman on the other end and that she was one of the people with whom he had spent his eventful summers with. I didn't know if she was a desired object of his, or if he was just being polite, but whatever responses were being regurgitated through the telephone receiver, they were enough to wet his palette and increase his confidence about attending the event.

Izzy wrestled the phone away from his ear, placed his hand over the talk area and asked:

"You wanna drive up or fly?"

"Where are we going?"

"Corning, NY!"

"Corning? Isn't that the name of the famous glass company?"

Izzy returned to his conversation and reserved our place at the party. When he placed the receiver back onto the base, he turned to me and said with a smile,

"Wow, how time flies! That woman on the phone was Kathleen Rozan!"

"Who is that? Is she related to the person you received the letter from?"

"Yes! That is his younger sister. Let me fill you in on the Quest-ors."

We sat at the table for the next three hours as Izzy took me on a fun-filled tour down memory lane and filled me in on the background of his suburban Chan Clan. He explained how they loved to watch the television cartoon 'Johnny Quest' in the afternoons, and how each of them would claim the rights of a character. He comically commented that somehow he always played Johnny's friend *Hadji*. I told him that maybe it was because of his striking good looks and gorgeous tan.

He went on to describe Kathleen as being tall and awkward for her age, with a mullet-type hairdo and huge saucer-plate bifocals. She lacked coordination and talked as if she was always gurgling on her saliva. Her mom forced her brother to look after her and to allow her play with the boys, because the other girls in the neighborhood would tease her and make her feel inferior. Unfortunately, she received even worse treatment from them, because she would always be cast as the monster to be slain or the relentless demon that just wouldn't die.

Her brother Mike was short, fat and nerdy. His parents called him 'Micro', which was a combo play on his original name, but it fit his demeanor like a glove. He loved anything to do with bugs, mammals or reptiles. He was an odd kid with reddish hair who was as smart as a professor and as funny as a prickly thorn bush. Most of the time, Micro would play Johnny's father, Dr. Benton Quest, because not only did he look like him, he also lacked the creativity and personality to be anyone else. Occasionally, though, he would ask to be the villain who controlled the monster. At first we thought it to be a bit weird, but this allowed him an avenue to seek retribution on Kathleen for whatever trouble she had gotten him in earlier in the week.

Graig Kerr was the super hyper kid that lived at the end of the street. He was always stuck on life-speed level nine and it didn't take much to send him into hyperspace. He was born with hair as black as the midnight sky, but desperately wanted to be a blond because he believed the advertisements that told him that blonds have more fun. He tried to dye his hair with a homemade remedy he concocted from a trashed inquirer magazine and the results were astonishing. Izzy said he looked like an excited Chia Pet but ironically, after he cut all of his hair off to minimize the damage, the area atop his head was noticeably lighter than his face, making him look kind of 'bald-blond-ish. Graig would ultimately resemble and become the group's magnanimous protector, Race Bannon.

Because everyone naturally wanted to be Johnny, to keep the peace, Izzy said that the group agreed to act as if the boy wonder would always be captured by the heartless villain or the vile, beastly monster. In doing so, each member of the group would have equal time to be the star for the day and the plot would always remain fresh and entertaining. That was a great idea, until Brett decided to come and crash the party. Brett was an older kid, who lived a few streets down and was an outcast from his own age group. Because he was a natural blond and physically bigger than anyone in the group, he would usually force himself into the role of Johnny Quest, but Izzy said his brash personality and egotistic demeanor made him resemble a different cartoon character named Johnny - *Johnny Bravo*.

During our five-hour journey northwest of the Big Apple, Izzy became perversely nostalgic and the stories began rolling off of his tongue like rain falling from a dark and stormy cloud. I found it quite amusing that he could recall all of these fond memories from his childhood, but couldn't remember what he ate for breakfast. I just sat back and played the passenger seat with the vigor of an anxious co-pilot and the intensity of a superhero's sidekick.

From the Holland Tunnel, across the northern part of New Jersey, winding through the State of Pennsylvania and on up towards Binghamton, the scenery was nothing short of fantastic. With the Michael Franks Pandora station providing the backdrop mood music, I couldn't help but feel as if I was meandering through an artist's rendition of heaven outlined by the subtleties of man. The majestic hillside home sites overlooking the valley of nature's incredible wonderland were eye-popping to say the least, and I could easily see how this indigenous window of life could be quite overwhelming for a young boy who mostly maneuvered through the shadows of grey concrete skyscrapers and chemically-stained foliage.

We continued onward through the City of Elmira and briefly stopped to pay homage to the fallen soldiers who lay eternally resting in Woodlawn National Cemetery. About a half hour later, we arrived in the city of Corning. I was feeling a bit weary from the long drive and famously starving from extreme hunger. With Izzy wanting to stop only for bathroom breaks so that we could utilize the daylight hours, our only food source had been what was individually packed within our respective luggage.

"I have to get something to eat. I'm beginning to hallucinate. Right now, with that crème colored blazer you have on, you look like a Nathan's hot dog to me."

Izzy smiled and parked the car in front of a restaurant on the main street. He jumped out and began looking around as if looking for something he lost in the air a long time ago. He took a deep breath and exclaimed,

"You smell that? You feel that? You sense that? This is what life without stress feels like. It's been such a long time since I have been here, but I feel as if I was destined to return."

I didn't want to spoil his sudden lust for life, but I was hungry and left him standing outside on the side walk as if he was waiting for a bus or something. I went into the restaurant and sat down like a normal patron. Izzy entered as if they would know who he was and it was tongue in cheek for me when he didn't receive the *'glad you are home'* reception from the waitress. Izzy began talking history with the waitress and explained that he used to visit during the summers of his childhood. The waitress then backs up, tilts her head sideways and stares sternly into Izzy's face.

"Hold the phone!" she says. "Were you one of the Fresh Air Fund kids who would get off the bus at the High School and stay in the community? "

"YES! YES, I AM!" said Izzy delightedly.

"Great! Welcome back - and by the way, you owe me five dollars."

"Excuse me. I owe you five dollars?"

"Sure do. Some years ago I was waiting this very table with a Fresh Air Fund family and they left a five dollar tip on the table but as they exited the restaurant their little visitor ran back and picked up my tip and ran out!"

The look on Izzy's face was *PRICELESS*! The waitress then told him to stand up and she hugged him tight like a mom cradling a frightened child. Her embrace opened the door for him to gently walk out from the midst of an awkward shadow of confusion by explaining it was all a joke. Izzy's huge sigh of relief was the signal for the remaining perpetrators to emerge from their hiding place. Within seconds, the kitchen door swung open and from the rear came the group of folks we were supposed to meet. Somehow, they had known Izzy would stop at this restaurant. Maybe it was a place he visited often as a child, and the swell of reminiscing during our travels were the bread crumbs that lured him to a familiar spot. Everyone seemed extremely excited to see us, and immediately they began hugging, crying and kissing Izzy as if they had just recovered a long-lost family member. The waitress led us towards the rear of the restaurant, where the larger tables were positioned for groups of people as wide as our party.

With Izzy seated perpendicular to the definitive dividing line of the big oval mahogany table, we all followed suit and puzzled ourselves into the open spaces around him. I will admit that the hunger which was being corralled inside my happy honeycomb of mannerisms began to become agitated and violently allergic to any type of friendly compromise. Hurriedly, I took the liberty to scan the restaurant's menu and open the discussion with the waitress about which dishes were not just quality but also high in quantity. She assured me that the portions would be sizable - more than enough to satisfy my needs, and anything that wasn't to our liking would be discarded and subtracted from our total bill. With that kind of guarantee tucked away in my back pocket, I couldn't help but take full advantage of the smorgasbord that was now readily at my disposal.

After our meal requests were committed to paper and submitted to the kitchen crew for preparation, our feisty caretaker politely bowed out of sight and allowed us to continue with our conversational contributions in an effort to mesh our dilapidated timeline.

"So Izzy, how does it feel to be back where it all began?" asked Micro.

With a smile as big as Texas, Izzy responded, "Wonderful and a bit nostalgic! It seems like just yesterday that the bus would pull into the high school and I would be sitting there waiting to be picked up and all the while wondering what time we had to wake up for swimming lessons. The water was so cold in the mornings that you had to get acclimatized by just jumping in. The big-toe-in-first test was just a huge waste of time."

"Do you remember the time we were at the pool and you fell asleep?" asked Graig.

"Oh, are you talking about the time you guys laughed at me because I woke up and saw chocolate feet?"

"That was hilarious; one of the funniest times I've ever experienced. Your sense of humor was always a priceless asset. You were always the coolest guy to be around. Everyone loved you and wanted to be like you. You always said the right things and told the best stories."

Kathleen chimed in with, "Yep, that's true. Remember when you showed up that year with that gigantic boom-box radio and introduced rap music to our inner circle? I can still hear that song. I bet I can still remember the lyrics: hip-hop, the hippy, the hippy-hippy-hip-hip-hop till you don't stop a rockin' to the bang-bang boogie, so up jump the boogie to the rhythm of the boogie the beat!"

Immediately the group raised their hands to shield their face as they attempted to tease Kathleen about the past and how she would project saliva when she spoke. We all began to fall deeper into a place of solemn solace and relaxed-shoulder peace. From the left side of my face, I could see our platters of food being stacked upon the wheeled transport tray and heading in our direction. The delicious aromas mixing and mingling on that small chariot were enough to cause a brief pause in their steadfast pursuit of the past. I opened both arms as wide as I could, hoping to receive my plate first and satisfy the need to feed the greed. I watched as the waitress placed my platter in the middle of my paper placemat, which advertised quick computer repair services and the designs of a local florist. She neatly placed my napkin across my lap and filled my glasses with ice water and green tea respectively. I was anxiously preparing myself to dive into the succulence of a well-prepared feast. With my silver fork resting in my right hand and a black-handled steak knife woven between the pointer and thumb of my left hand, I began to slice off a piece of heaven and plunge it into my cavernous tomb filled with saliva and thirty-two white porcelain teeth. I closed my eyes briefly in a selfish attempt to shut off the other four senses, but before I could unplug and enjoy my meal, I heard:

"You know what the best was? Remember the times when we would be just sitting around and he would tell the scary stories? Street monsters, crack addicts, rats and other city stuff - but my absolute favorite was about the Tall Man with the leather jacket and the hat that matched. Yep, that was the best. The way you used to tell that story made me jump because it felt so real! I'm getting chills just thinking about it. How did you come up with that?"

My eyes sprung open and took a hard turn towards Izzy. My mind went into a scramble mode and my heart sunk into my shoes. Izzy looked at me with a surprised look of guilt and gently raised his hand above the table signaling to me that he would answer this but not before I was able to

comically blurt out:

"...natural-born story-teller."

CHAPTER 14:
ACTIVE IMAGINATIONS

"...I don't want to be the monster anymore! Why can't I be Johnny's sister or

something?"

"If you want to continue playing with us, then you gotta play your part. Besides, Johnny

doesn't have a sister...and unfortunately I DO! You can always go down the street and play with

the other girls, Kathleen. I'm sure they would be glad to have you join them."

"Oh, shut up, Micro! You know I can't play with them. Let's do something different for a

change."

"Different like what?"

"I know! Let's take Izzy down by the river where Old Man Jones lives. I bet it will scare

the pants off of him."

"What's so scary about Old Man Jones?"

"Old Man Jones is a vampire!"

"A WHAT?"

"Yeah, you heard right! He's a blood sucker!"

"Ok. You've been watching way too many channel five movies."

"Izzy, I'm serious! When he first showed up in town 16 years ago, he had

moved in with Ms. Whitehead who used to live next door. We used to hear screams at night when the moon was full and one day, Ms. Whitehead came over to the house to borrow a cup of sugar and my mom noticed two mysterious red marks on the side of her neck. Then, at the neighborhood picnic, Ms. Whitehead was bitten by a snake and fell to the ground. Instead of calling 9-1-1, Old Man Jones couldn't resist the urge to drink her blood so he rushed over and started sucking her leg like a crazed demon. Shortly after that, Ms. Whitehead disappeared and Old Man Jones moved into the raggedy old place by the lake. He has never has any visitors, nor does he ever come out of the house - during the day, that is. It's been said that some kids were down by the lake skinny-dipping one night and were attacked by someone with long fangs and dark eyes. That's why we lock our doors and windows up tight at night!"

"Who told you this? We weren't even born 16 years ago?"

"It's true! If he catches you and bites your neck, you become one of them. You are safe during the day, but at night, he flies around in search of victims. We see more bats around here than ever before. I bet Ms. Whitehead is one of them because once a week, one will hang upside down from the side of the roof next door. Out of all the houses on this street, why do you think it picked the one next door? I think it's her coming back home."

"You know what I think?"

"What?"

"Old Man Jones may be you guys' daddy! You know, ever since I have been coming out here, I have never met your father. Didn't you say he was a pilot?"

"Har-dee-har-har! Izzy, that wasn't so funny! Old Man Jones is **REAL**! Micro, please tell him."

"It's true, man. I don't know what types of monsters live in the city, but out here, we have the real stuff!"

"Well, truth be told, my best friend LIVES with a monster."

"For real?"

"Yeah, a cold-blooded killer!"

"You ever see him kill anyone?"

"Yeah, well sought of."

"Tell us about it!"

"Well, one night while staying at one of my friends' houses, we decided to join the rest of our group and go see a movie. We had basically spent the entire day in the house and were beginning to get a little claustrophobic from being confined all day. My friend's mom had spent the evening at a family member's home so it was just the two of us and his mom's boyfriend. We got ourselves ready and headed for the door. As I passed the sofa, I accidently knocked over a rust-colored leather jacket and matching leather hat that was draped over the back. I bent down to pick it up, apologizing throughout my motions, and as I was returning to an upright stance, I saw a look of frozen fear pasted upon his face. I looked at him sideways, reminding him that it was only a jacket. As we were exiting his apartment, we overheard a loud but muffled yell, then the sound of a phone being slammed down on its base. I didn't think much of it at the time - I figured it was something to do with Uncle Al again and proceeded to walk out of the door, down the square stairwell, past the community mailboxes and into the night air.

"Uncle AL? Why would he be talking to YOUR Uncle?"

"Uh, well since we were like brothers, we would refer to each other's family as our own."

"Be quiet Kathleen! Stop interrupting! Go ahead Izzy...finish."

"Our brilliant plan to pay for two people to go into separate theaters and then open the side doors for the rest of us to get in was flawless. Given the benefit of doubt that we chose the right two people to carry out the plan, we would have money for popcorn, drinks and candy. After we bum-rushed our way inside, we discovered that someone from our neighborhood was working the refreshment stand. Our experience became an all you could eat buffet for the price of another ticket. We thought we had just hit the jackpot and decided to stay and see as many movies as we could. About twenty minutes into the movie, my best friend began to fidget and squirm around in his seat noticeably. I asked him what the problem was and he responded that the movie was boring! I looked around and saw that the entire theater was packed and everyone was enjoying the film, then looked back at him like he was crazy. I didn't say anything and went back to watching the movie. Another twenty minutes passed and he suddenly got up. I asked him again what was wrong and he responded this time by saying he had to go home. For the life of me I couldn't understand why he would want to leave this perfect setup we just maneuvered ourselves into, but he was extremely uneasy and seemed to be getting more agitated the more everyone threw out sales pitches for him to stay. Because we came together, we had to leave together, so his wanting to go meant that I was done too. Most of our money was used on the candy buffet, so we couldn't catch a cab back home. We walked quickly down the street and I noticed that my friend was going faster than normal. I figured that whatever it was that was making him want to go home so bad, was important. After leaving the movies, walking past the bus stop and continuously taking an extra step just to keep up, I could tell that we would be walking the seven-mile trip back home. We walked about a half of a mile without talking. I asked him again what the problem was and he finally answered. He told me that he had a gut feeling that something was terribly wrong at home. It was really weird, because he told me that it felt as if someone was sitting in his chair with him, pushing him from behind and trying to make him get up and rush home immediately. We walked roughly another mile and I wanted to rest. I was really thirsty because of all that salty food that I had been eating in the theater. We went off into a corner bodega...."

"What is a bodega?"

"It's what we call the small family-owned stores that usually are on the corners of every community in the city."

"Oh. Why are you staring at me like that, Micro?"

"Anyway, we kept moving and my friend never slowed down at all. Whatever was driving him at that moment was much more than I had ever seen before. He was focused and determined to get home as fast as possible, but he couldn't really explain why. About an hour later, we passed the elementary school that we both attended. I tried to make a joke by reminding him about a time when we were being wild and mischievous. We would always ring this bell to one of the warehouses on our way to school then run away. One day, I wanted to mix it up and ring a second bell, but I was too small to reach it. So I had my buddy lift me as the other boys watched and while pushing the bell, a bee flew up my pants leg and stung me on my left thigh. He laughed at me all day, saying that I looked like I was being electrocuted the way I was flapping my arms around and yelling for him to put me down. Usually this would have at least gotten him to smirk or chuckle, but not this time. Ten minutes later, we turned onto one of the streets around our housing complex. There was an arcade and pool hall on the corner, and as we went past, we looked through the big bay window and he noticed someone he knew, so we turned back and went inside. His cousin was playing the video game Space invaders and he walked over to her and asked how long had she been there. She told him that they had come about an hour ago. Then, he asked where his mom was and she told him that his mom was at the house. He took a step back and ran out of the building as if it was on fire. I trailed in the dust that he kicked up behind him and by this time I was petrified because I didn't know what was going on. We ran through the block jumping over park benches, dodging neighbors and their enormous dogs, parked cars and rocks that were being thrown by other kids. We were locked onto our target, which was his apartment, and there was absolutely nothing that was going to stop us from reaching it. When we hit *the front door of the building, the door was locked and we didn't have the*

key to get in. He began banging on the intercom system, which only worked

sometimes, hoping that someone would be annoyed with it enough that

they would click their own entry button and buzz him in. Now that I think

about it, I don't know why he didn't just ring his own apartment, but I guess

adrenaline had taken over or maybe he was calling for help before he

actually knew why. After we did that for a minute, someone in the building

hit the release button from their apartment's intercom system so we could

open the heavy metal door and go in. From here, it looked as if I was

walking behind a detective in the crime scene of a movie. We began to walk

up the first set of steps, and wound up on the first floor. Holding onto the

railing with our left hands, we swung around and began walking up the

second pair of steps. We had our right hands pressed up tight against the

wall so we could jump through the third stair casing, but he slipped on the

blood that was smeared on the wall and I fell on top of him. We were so

high on adrenaline that we kept going, regardless of any damaged egos or

body parts. I looked down noticed his right hand was covered in blood. I

tapped him on the back to let him know, but he was already locked in on the

trail of blood which led from the stairwell onto the second floor and into his

apartment. We stood very cautiously in front of his apartment and saw that

the front door was slightly cracked open. He pushed forward and walked into what looked like a bomb had gone off. Everything was either out of

place, turned over or broken. My friend cupped his mouth with his hands

and began to call out to his mom. I reached out and put both hands on his

shoulders and slowly walked with him towards the back of the apartment.

He called out to her again, a bit like a lost pup who strayed away from the

litter, but there was still no response. We were trying to be ready for the

worst, but nothing could ever prepare you for what we were about to see.

There are so many violent acts that occur in the crowded city every day, but

you couldn't imagine how scared and stressed you get when it is happening

to YOU. We walked carefully past his room and were surprised that it was

the only room in the place that was not touched; it was exactly as we had

left it. We could tell we were right, because my friend had a clear-coated

string tied to the bottom of his bedpost and then connected the opposite end

to the small wooden splinters that would form at the bottom of his door,

and it wasn't broken. Another five steps and we were standing in front of his

mother's bedroom door, which was a little warped. We stood there for a

moment not knowing what to expect. All sorts of hideous thoughts were

running through our minds. On the other side of this wooden divider, we

knew that we would find the answer to all of our questions, and the reason

for the gut feeling that made us leave the movie theatre and pulled us to

that very spot. My buddy reached out to turn the door knob, but he was so scared that he couldn't move his wrist. I put my hand over his and turned the knob until I heard a click. I pushed the door open slowly, and what we saw made our eyes fall low and our stomachs even lower. We could see a large pool of dark red blood at the foot of the bed. In the puddle was the antique bamboo walking stick, which was about as thick as a table leg. It was completely splintered in half and it seemed as if its insides were slowly releasing the final squirts of blood before it died. We scoured the room with wide eyes and our jaws dropped when we saw how the displaced furniture gave away what had happened. My friend became overwhelmed with grief as his brain began to process the thought of life without a parent and he fell onto the bed, with his hands over his eyes and his feet in the pool of blood. I suddenly jumped a few steps backwards when I felt the wiggle of something beneath my left foot. I heard a muffled crunch of glass and when I reached down to check what it was, I found the remains of a charred smoking pipe. I immediately yelled to my buddy demanding him to stand and shouted, "Let's get out of here!" I helped him from the foot of the bed and together we walked back through the mess and out the front door. Our blood-stained sneaker prints followed us toward help until our cries were heard by a neighbor who motioned for us to come inside her apartment. We kept holding onto each other as if we were Siamese twins, and walked across her doorway and threw ourselves into the two front chairs at her dining room *table. After we caught our breath and lifted our heads to speak, we noticed*

someone sprawled out on her couch with a white towel with red spots across

their head. We both looked at each other and as my friend got up to go

uncover the truth, his neighbor bear-hugged him to try and comfort him

while the paramedics worked to get the injured person ready for hospital

transport. I remember the look on my best friend's face as they drove away.

I was standing a few feet away from him as he was still being wrapped up in

the neighbor's arms. He cut his eyes at me, squinted, and clenched his lips

before mouthing: "I'm going to kill him". I remember that, because that was

when the innocence of my friend died and I knew he had changed forever.

He wasn't the happy-go-lucky guy I was used to anymore. What I saw was

the birth of something more sinister, with growing levels of rage, and I could

tell that revenge was the only thing making his heart beat."

"Wow Izzy, that's kind of frightening!"

"Yeah man, it sure is. Is he still a buddy? What happened to him in

the end?"

"Oh, he's cool; just taking it one day at a time. We still keep in touch

almost daily because I'm the only one who can relate to what he has gone

through."

"So Dr. Quest, why don't we continue our journey to save Johnny by slaying this hideous monster? Let me get my sword and shield."

"Ok, Hadji! Let's sneak up on it and cut off its head!"

"Mom! The boys are ganging up on me again!"

"Oh no! Catch her before she goes in the house and tells my mom. I'll be in trouble...AGAIN! KATHLEEN, COME BACK! WE WERE JUST KIDDING!"

CHAPTER 15:
GREAT IDEAS

It had been a few weeks since we returned home from our fantastic voyage to Never-Never Land and interacted with its extremely hospitable inhabitants who treated us like traditional English royalty. Since our return home, I had begun to see subtle changes in Izzy's demeanor. He seemed more cheerful than he had in recent months. His repertoire of facial expressions and non-verbal communications had been on full display, producing an abundance of wide-mouthed smiles and bucketsful of joyful gestures. I'm not saying that he was as happy as a Diamond Amway representative, but he was showing more of a zest for life.

The more I sat thinking about his metamorphism from ticking tragedy to opulent optimistic, it became abundantly clear to me that my best friend needed to be able to inhale a breath of fresh air deep into his lungs, exhale the mucus of its unwanted characteristics, then revel in the aftermath of translucency. If his Fresh Air Fund experiences afforded him a higher level of peace and clarity, then it only made sense to spend most of his time in that happy place. He deserved that, after all that he had been through - and maybe I was being a little selfish here, but I could have used a vacation from my one-patient psychological practice.

I decided to contact the rest of the group so that we could tell them about our adventure and allow Izzy some additional opportunity of reflection through explanation. Getting the group together and receiving an infusion of their daily plights is always a joyful occasion for Izzy. I know he always thought of us as more than close friends. I would go as far as brothers, but we all know that even close siblings have their own unwritten dos and don'ts regarding one another.

The first call I made was to Calvin. I explained to him what I was thinking and what I was trying to accomplish for Izzy and as soon as I paused, he seized the opportunity and jumped right in with his ideas. Izzy always said to know your personnel and I knew that calling Calvin would send his circuits into overdrive. I knew that he would not only take the idea and make it his own, but somehow, someway, Triple C would put the plan in motion - not always heading in the right direction, but definitely in motion.

Once I had confirmation that Calvin was on board, I reached out to David. The phone rang several times before activating the voicemail message. I looked down at my watch to see what time it was, and realized that David was still in class conducting lessons. I didn't want to leave a message, so I decided to hang up and call Gus. Upon the initial ring, a young woman answered the call:

"Hello?"

"Gus?" I replied.

"Um, no... Who is this?"

"I'm sorry, I must have dialed the wrong number. I was looking for my friend."

I hung up the phone and dialed Gus' number slowly. Again, it was picked up on the first ring:

"Helllllloooo...?"

It was the same young woman's voice from the previous call. She was popping chewing gum in my ear so hard that I thought she was about to injure her bottom jawbone. I explained to her that I was in search of my friend Gustavo and that until just recently this was his phone number. She said she did not know anyone by the name of Gustavo. Immediately, I heard a familiar voice yelling in the background then a slight tussle taking place on the other end of the phone. Gus spoke an apologetic greeting into the receiver and awaited confirmation of who was holding the other line. As an old school guy, he still had his initial phone from 1993...a flip-phone without a caller ID.

"Hey man, it's me!" I said.

"Oh! Wassup, dude? When did you guys get back?"

Before I continued with that line of conversation, I had to rip on him about the young voice on the other end of the phone.

"Who was that who answered your phone?"

"Oh, her? Nobody, just a friend of mine."

"A friend, huh? How old is this friend?"

"She's twenty-four, but she is a mature twenty four…"

"There is no such thing as a mature twenty-four. Where did you meet her…at a Nickelodeon taping? Or did the yellow school bus break down again on your way to work? These young women are gonna be the death of you someday. You can't keep buying bubble gum and penny candies to catch a date. Step your game up before someone calls the department of Child Protective Services on you!"

Gus took the ribbing like water off a ducks back. It is not like this is the first time he has heard this from one of us. I started to tell him about the gathering I wanted to put together for Izzy. As always, he responded in a completely supportive manner and asked what we needed him to do. I told him that Triple C would be making all the arrangements and would let us know the details, but the first thing we would need from him was a commitment to stop hanging around with people who watch Sponge Bob and eat Crabby Patties. He let out a little chuckle and then replied

sarcastically in his thick Caribbean accent:

"You know what, you're right. I am going to stop this madness of

having fun and chasing beautiful women who are naturally in shape, with no

overblown relationship or credit issues and robustly career-oriented. I

understand that according to you and the rest of society, I need to grow up

and deal with women my age who have tons of baby-daddy drama, mad at

the world because of the repeated bad life choices they make and with no

positive outlook anywhere in sight. You're right buddy, I'd be much happier

in that pool of wickedness."

Gus has a way of being truthfully sarcastic. It's what I believe to be

his unique and vivacious quality that he brings to the group. He has always

run behind the younger ladies, looking for his special supermodel who

drinks from the fountain of youth - and one day I hope he finds her, but this

is not about Gus nor his playpen playmate. This is about the energy and

organic elation amongst our group and the willingness to laser-like focus

that joy into Izzy's heart.

With three of the four members of our group onboard and in

agreement, the remaining task was to call David again. I picked up my

phone to dial his number and realized that I had a missed call. The number on the caller ID was not familiar to me so I decided to listen to the voicemail message before proceeding:

"Hey, this is Davey. Saw that you called but I was busy working on the new routines for the upcoming show. Hope all went well with the trip. Call me. I want to hear all about it."

I quickly hit redial on my phone.

Davey answered after two rings and we routinely exchanged gleeful greetings and methodical pleasantries before leveling off and focusing our attention on Izzy.

"How is he doing?" asked David.

"Better! He seems to be on an emotional upswing and the trip really helped him crawl from underneath the blanket of pity. I'm not sure if he has put it totally behind him yet but he's moving in the right direction."

"That's great! I continue to pray for my brother every day."

We both stood idle for a moment with the phone receivers pressed up against our earlobes as if we were silently paying homage to someone who was no longer with us. It was an awkward moment in time and I knew Davey was quick to get emotional, so I abruptly blurted out our plans:

"Well, this is why I wanted to reach out to you buddy. The group is putting together a little appreciation party for Izzy so that we can publicly show our love for him and our loyalty as brothers. But truth be told, the more I think about it, we all could use a dose of pick-me-up."

"I agree! You know I'm in. Just let me know when and where."

I hung up the phone with an intense feeling of progression and anticipation. Getting the guys together and catching up would be totally awesome. One thing that we truly understood was that life may have her sons spread out in space with their own set of planetary issues and concerns, but we always realized that we are part of a larger entity and at certain times, it was crucial to replenish the energy source that fueled the galaxy.

Two weeks later I found myself sitting in front of the computer in my office. The chic multi-pattern designed windows were cracked open and a gentle breeze began surfing across the horizon of my textured glass desk, underneath the multiple stacks of eight-and-a-half by eleven-inch note paper, then suddenly decided to wipeout. The invisible catalyst caused a stir that garnered an immobilized pause from me. Mentally, it made me revisit Izzy's stage misstep. The thirty-three muscles in my face began vying for elbow room and their irritable discontent stoned an egregious look as I watched what I believed to be an uncanny piece of a *De Ja Vu*. Violently, the

top layers of my skin became riddled with a sea of goose bumps and the fine

hairs that lined my forearms magically began to levitate. The cool air which

was now surrounding my person accentuated the chilling feeling I was

experiencing at that very moment. The broken stacks of paper leaping from

the confines of my desktop, individually exhibiting their resistance with the

laws of gravity, blanketed my vision to the outside world and all I could see

was pocketed moments of Izzy's fall from grace.

Faintly in the background, I heard a growing noise as if someone

decided that this was where the score of the movie fitted in. A familiar

melodic jingle interrupted my nonalcoholic inebriated state, being enough

to reverse the trance-like scene I had become trapped in. The newly-

awakened pupils of my squinted eyes and the anorexic lobes of my

imperfectly carved ears quickly became viable search engines, scanning the

room for the origin of the sound. I swiveled my billionaire black captain's

chair ninety degrees east, then with both hands gripped tightly upon the

padded armrests, I rocketed myself north and navigated towards the front

door.

I stood there watching the door as if I was looking into a mirror with

no reflection. I awaited another ring from the doorbell to give me confirmation that I was fully awake from my daydream. Seconds later, there was a knock.

"Who is it?" I asked.

"It is Fletcher sir. Are you alright? We placed a call from the lobby to inform you that you have a visitor, but we received no response. I knew you were here as I saw your car this morning. I just wanted to make sure you were okay."

"A visitor? What kind of visitor, Fletcher?"

"A female, sir. She says her name is Medusa. She is quite attractive and charming. Should I send her up?"

I reached down, grabbed the metal doorknob and turned it clockwise to give Fletcher a clear, unobstructed view of my person. He had been the doorman at my apartment building for years and he had become like a surrogate older brother to me. I wanted to look into his baggy green eyes and see the expressions on his gray bearded face, as I was unsure who this Medusa person was.

"Hey, man. Thanks for checking on me. I guess you can send her up. Hopefully I don't have a hit out on me. Did you pat her down first?"

Fletcher looked back at me and chuckled with what I pegged to be his Marvel Comics super-villain grin, which showed all twenty eight of his teeth. A year ago, he could have been a denture model, but there had been a domestic disturbance in the lobby area in which he tried to mitigate and during the chaos, he lost four of his "chicklets".

"Mentally I did, but I don't need my fifteen minutes of fame to be displayed on the News Channels as the dirty doorman from downtown! I'll send her right up."

Fletcher stepped onto the elevator and shrugged his shoulders at me just before the sliding door severed our visual connection. My mental rolodex was spinning at a feverish pace trying to place a face with the name. I was consistently falling short as I couldn't recall ever meeting anyone named Medusa. I stood befuddled in the doorway to the apartment, hoping for the best but anticipating the worst.

I looked up at the digital display just above the elevator door and stared upon its rising numbers...six, seven, eight, nine...***DING!*** As the elevator lift car reached the tenth floor and tucked away its sliding door, a goddess emerged from the shadows. Walking towards me in a way that is usually reserved for the runway, this bi-racial brunette exuded sassy sex appeal. With her honeycomb skin tone wrapped tightly in a lustful red miniskirt, I could do nothing but stare. I soon understood why she had the name Medusa, because my midsection was turning to stone quickly. The closer she got to me, the more aware I became that this woman was "about something". She stopped in front of my apartment with her hands placed strategically on her hips and her red-bottomed Christian Louboutins about shoulder width apart. I momentarily fell in lust until she began to sing, utilizing Rosie Perez's vocal tones.

"Hello there, it's so nice to meet you;

A friend of yours sent me to personally greet you

And invite you to an exclusive event downtown,

For a man who fell down and almost broke his crown.

His recovery is the reason we choose to celebrate,

So make sure you R.S.V.P before it gets too late;

I sure hope you will join us and share in the joy

That will be shared amongst the group, your best friends, and your boys!"

She placed a black velvet envelope into my hand, gave me a hug, then turned around and headed for the elevator. I stood there, stunned, with my jaw dropped, trying to make sense of what had just occurred. Once she was committed to memory, I closed the door to my apartment, picked up my cell phone and began dialing.

"*What was that?*" I asked.

"*Oh, I see you've met Medusa! How'd it feel being turned to stone? She's part of my new business venture called* **Musi-Cal Girls**.

"*Triple C, you are definitely cooky, cocky and crazy!*

CHAPTER 16:
INFECTIOUS ACQUAINTANCES

I received a group text message from Calvin demanding that we all meet him in front of Madison Square Garden at seven o'clock. He claimed that he scored some great Knicks tickets and it had been some time since we all went to a game together. I was actually a little skeptical about the idea, but once again, I was trying to take Izzy's advice and be a little more positive in my thinking. When it came to Calvin and his "ideas", my spider senses usually flared up like a bad case of hemorrhoids - and this time was no different.

Izzy and I were already in the midtown area after finishing our client meeting a little earlier than expected, so we decided to head over to Eighth Avenue and have a drink at one of the local bars. Surprisingly, we were able to hail a cab on the first try and even got a, "Good afternoon, gentlemen," from our European tour driver before we started our trek across town. After a few minutes of window-framing bone-colored concrete and gray steel from the backseat of our four-wheeled chariot for hire, I leaned over towards Izzy and made a joke about Calvin's spontaneous request and how his past undertakings had typically been adventures that became moments of high regret.

Izzy chuckled and nodded his head in agreement.

I took a moment to breathe, then decided to change the topic of our discussion from Calvin's kooky adventures to the return of life as WE knew it. I commented on how great it was to feel his smiling persona again and gloated on his decision to once again allow the joys of life to invade his protected personal space. Slowly, he turned his head one hundred and eighty degrees, tilted it slightly and placed his chin gently into the palm of his left hand. With four fingers cascaded from just under the bottom of his right earlobe to the corner of his nose, he responded,

"I have begun the much-needed journey to successfully untangle the cobwebs of thought that have been occupying my mind. I am excited about what is on the horizon in the very near future. An adjustment of my internal telescopic lenses have forced me to re-evaluate my perspective on life and conclude a quotient to the original equation that has been rendering me divided."

"Awesome!" I replied. "So, the trip down memory lane was successful in more ways than one?"

"Yes. It helped regurgitate something I had read some time ago, but had not digested its true meaning into my DNA until a few weeks ago."

"Cool. Care to share?"

He took a moment to focus his vision back towards the high-definition moving pictures that were being displayed through the rectangular window of the taxicab. The cool breeze blowing back into his face muffled his response a bit, but I could make out what was being said:

"Our brains are the control room to all that we do and serve as the catalysts to every individual experience. What we feel; what we see; what we taste, touch and smell; are all regulated from a piece of matter that occupies roughly twelve hundred cubic centimeters of space and weighs approximately three pounds. Much like the most complex processor residing within the latest computer, it functions like an autonomous entity whereby sometimes it experiences glitches within its matrix. When we spoke in the hospital a few months ago, my internal computer chip was operating from the vantage point of a soldier ant within a colony of millions. My emotions were controlling my movements and thoughts and because I couldn't get out of my own way, I was nose-diving into a death roll. I was unable to lift my eyes from my capitated surroundings to see the big picture. All of my positive energy was on an extended vacation and threatening to relocate for good, but the spontaneous trip we took allowed me to briefly escape the emotional enclosure and sparked my imagination to once again come alive. Revisiting a time in my life when my make-believe was more important than

my reality, encouraged the emergence of a new path to walk upon. So, no

longer will I only focus on the backside of the soldier ant directly in front of

me. This two-toned caterpillar has cocooned himself to blossom into a

multi-colored butterfly and change the angles of his perspective to see life's

bigger picture - which happens to fit a lot better within my personal

screenplay."

Remarkably, I understood the words that were being sent in my direction, but it took a minute for its meaning to become embedded in my mind. The vehicular vocabulary that was being expelled through the air in the rear cabin of the cab floated into the dark depths of my left ear, down my auditory canal and pounced on my eardrum until the vibrations became electrical signals that my brain could read, but somewhere along the process, those signals collided with a black and red detour sign which redirected them to the nearest exit - which happened to be across the semi-spherical room. A bewildered stare and sudden eye flutter must have exposed my inner comprehensive confusion, because it prompted Izzy to close his eyes and slowly ingest a chest full of manufactured wind and before exhaling it through his flared nostrils, he displayed his signature sixteen-tooth grin followed by a subtle east to west repetitive head shake.

A few minutes later, our cab ride came to an end in the bus only lane on the corner of Eighth Avenue and Thirty-Fourth Street. We exited just in front of the New Yorker Hotel after pleasantly tipping our driver handsomely for his showmanship of equality. As my shoes hit the ground and I erected my body towards the heavens, I noticed a folded green one-hundred dollar bill. Instincts forced me to silently place my left foot on it and bend down to retie my shoe. Izzy kept moving ahead, but the hot dog vendor with the blue and yellow Sabrett awning looked me dead in my eyes and belted out a laugh loud enough to communicate to me what he saw but secret enough to blend in with the movements of everyday Manhattan rush hour. I picked up the folded fortune and placed it into my right pocket and patted it twice before hurrying my steps to catch my buddy.

I followed him across the rough terrain of Eighth Avenue, dodging oncoming cars, day walkers and men on yellow mountain bikes with an elongated double-passenger bench seat attached. Once safe atop the other side of the raised walkway, we decided our destination should be T.G.I.F.'s. I pulled the glass door towards my chest and held it open for Izzy to pass through, then continued holding for some exiting patrons before releasing my grip as I jumped across the silver grid plate housed at the bottom of the door jamb. We walked in and were immediately seated upstairs at a dimly-lit corner table that gave us a heightened panoramic view of the often chaotic human combustion that occurs within the multiple intersections of Eighth Avenue and Thirty-Fourth Street.

Our table hostess was an attractive woman with the physique of a retired dancer. Her legs seemed to go on forever and her waistline would have made you think that she was not being compensated fairly. She wore her hair in a short cut style, which allowed her big beautiful brown eyes to say hello before she verbally spoke a word. She stood in the background with no one to hide behind and squinted her face to focus her vision. She grabbed a menu then approached our table cautiously.

"Excuse me for the stare, but you look so familiar," she informed us.

Izzy replied, *"No, I don't believe we have ever met before."*

"Please forgive me, sir, I am usually good about putting names and faces together, but I feel so sure that I have met you before."

Izzy wasn't sure if her attempt at creating personable dialog was an icebreaker for additional conversation or just her way of running a routine to prep her patrons for a bigger tip. He smiled at her with a corporate professional face and then verbally opened the door for her to expose her true intentions:

"I've been told before that I resemble a few folks that walk these perimeters and maybe I do have a face that can jog a memory, but I am

quite certain that we have not crossed paths before. Do you live here in the city?"

"I live uptown now but I grew up just over the bridge."

"Which bridge?" said Izzy.

"The Queensboro Bridge. What would you like to drink?"

I could see Izzy's antenna's becoming stimulated and he wanted to press the conversation a bit further but was compelled to fall back. We both wondered who this girl was and how she could have known him. She took our entire order without committing one word to paper. Clearly, she was more talented than what we were witnessing on the surface and to peel back the layers to uncover the details was something we were not willing to thrust ourselves into at this moment. Heck, if this seemingly attractive woman was not remembered by either one of us, then she must not have been an important figure in our past and whatever path led her to waiting tables here must have been one filled with a boatload of drama and that was exactly what we did not need in our lives right now.

Ten minutes later, she returned to our table with a look of sheer gratification.

"I think I have figured it out. You used to ride the Greyhound bus as a Fresh Air kid right?"

Izzy sat back in his chair filled with intrigue.

"Yes, I did."

"That is how we know each other. I was on that bus taking that five hour ride every summer. One year we were sitting next to each other, back then I was pudgy with braces across the top row of my teeth, I was trying to shove food down my fat face before the other kids would ask me for some and a short time later, I shared my food with your shirt."

"That was you?"

"Yeah. I am so sorry for ruining your clothes that day. I just knew you hated my guts! My name is Andrea by the way."

"I'm Israel."

"Nice to meet you Israel. I'll be right back with your food."

Andrea turned and walked away with a new sense of accomplishment and Izzy felt a bit ashamed as now the true story of the infamous tie dye shirt had been revealed. I was bent over laughing hysterically as I envisioned him sitting in his unwavering corporate persona, but just beneath the lining of his suit jacket was a tight tie-dye shirt made from heckled saliva, stale mashed potatoes and regurgitated brown gravy. I felt Izzy's eyes tearing me to shreds from a distance, but for the next ten minutes, I repelled all incoming signals - both verbal and nonverbal, as I was severely drowning in a comical stupor.

Once we corralled our emotions and moved past the comedy hour, we satisfied our bellies and lined our throats with foods and beverages that would surely come back to haunt us in the very near future. It's something to be said for people over a certain age to be consuming foods that contain gluten. The path it takes to travel throughout the body is tumultuous to say the least and its exit strategy is as powerful as a sperm whale's blowhole. The return of Andrea to our table was the final call for refills and the introduction of the bill. I immediately reached out and took control of the white and black receipt, then laid my debit card down to complete the transaction.

"Hey bro, why don't you pay with cash so that she can receive her tip right away" said Izzy.

"Ok. I'll leave her an extra special tip as well as she was great and I enjoyed the conversation."

Andrea came by and picked up the black bill tray and began clearing our table. She was really appreciative of the gratuity I chose to leave behind and gave me a hug as a result. I was feeling pretty good after getting that type of response from a beautiful lady such as that and asked her if I could call her and possibly have dinner. She agreed, grabbed my phone and put her telephone number in my contacts along with a selfie so that I wouldn't forget her. As we left the restaurant, I was grinning harder than a Cheshire cat.

"Hey dude, I'm glad you found humor in her story about our one and only dinner date" said Izzy.

"It was very funny bro. Don't be ashamed. Your secret is safe with me."

We walked across Eighth Avenue and saw Gus and Davey standing in front of Madison Square Garden. A few minutes later, Calvin appeared with his new acquaintance, who was responsible for gifting him the tickets. We all shook hands and thanked Mr. Pennar collectively for his generosity. We began our trek towards the entrance of the Garden, when Izzy suddenly turned to me with an apologetic poker face and said,

"Oh, by the way, I hope you didn't use that one hundred dollar bill that was laying on the ground to pay for our meal. As far as I could

remember, President Franklin does not show his two front teeth and sport a hoop earring."

My heart sunk all the way to my toes, completed a reverse summersault and tied my shoes. Izzy patted me on my back and winked his eye as I stood on the curb wrestling with the idea on how he played me like a violin. He caught up with the guys and headed into the building as I took off running in the opposite direction. Not only do I have to face Andrea about the counterfeit bill, I have to try and keep myself from being arrested.

About thirty minutes later, I was able to find my way inside Madison Square Garden and as I joined the group, I began to get ribbed about carrying Hip-Hop money. Everyone seemed to have their own joke about it, even the new guy. I took the verbal lashings with a grain of salt and dismissed it like water off of a duck's back. It had been such a long time since we sat in the seats of the world's most famous arena and I wasn't going to let a little thing like that spoil my night.

During the pregame shoot around, Gus leaned over and asked Mr. Pennar how he met Calvin. Pennar boasted that he owned his own company called M.O.P Fragrances and that he had met Calvin during a black-and-white tie affair. He dug into the inside left pocket of his blue-and-orange Knickerbockers jacket and pulled out a business card to hand each of us. Morris Oliver Pennar, President and CEO. Calvin leaned over and chimed in with all the great business deals that M.O.P. had been involved with throughout the past three years and how this new joint venture would be the start of a rolling empire. Izzy looked at me, I looked at Gus - and we all looked at David, who was enjoying himself by dancing in the isle to Lionel Richie's *'All Night Long',* which was blasting from the overhead speakers. Gus let out a huge sigh before saying, *"Some things never change."*

And with that acknowledgement, so too came the horn to start the game. This was closely followed by the ill-timed rise of gas bubbles deep within our midsections, warning us that it was now time to release dinner.

CHAPTER 17:
FADE TO BLACK

It was nine-fifteen and no one had heard anything from the driver. With the weather abusively beating at the window panes and the sharp flashes of light illuminating the city, it was feasible to assume that our mode of transportation may be altered at some point in the near future. At the time, it seemed like a fantastic idea to facilitate a chauffeured limousine to usher in the guest of honor and his makeshift entourage, but alas, there we sat in disarray as another of Calvin's diamond jewels ended up being "*cubic-zirconiated.*"

With the weight of the stone-colored wall leaning up against his broad left shoulder and his eyes fixated on some alluring entity on the other side of the glass, my best buddy looked as if he was striking a pose for the next cover of GQ magazine. Dressed in an obsidian black Calvin Klein Mirage 2-button notched tuxedo, cloaked over a classic white monogrammed lay down Gitman shirt with sparkling black diamond cuff links and a Sean John Baltic black silk bow tie, Izzy's attire spawned admirable glares from his successful three-man crew, which were reflected within the streaks of the translucent glass.

I scoured the room with a predator-like silence as each member of the group found their own way to preoccupy themselves. The additional time brought about by a non-responsive chariot allowed me to sit back and observe how far we all had come and how time had chosen to age our stature whilst preserving our boyish personas.

Calvin paced up and down the middle of the room, his Johnston and Murphy Cap Toe Oxfords gently scrubbing the nylon fibers within the area rug and leaving an imbedded imprint as he shifted his weight from one foot to another. Glowing underneath an ivory-white two-button lapel tuxedo jacket with flap pockets draped seamlessly over a pair of onyx black pleated dress pants, walking in a

cemented seven step turn and repeat scheme, he began to dig deep into his mental reservoir of names, searching for a way to resuscitate his failed attempt at giving Izzy the grandiose entrance he had planned. Knowing Calvin the way I did, I had bet he was also in search of the shiny silver lining within this dark cloud to grab ahold of, package it and ultimately benefit from.

On the right side of the room, opposite of where Izzy was posing for pictures, I could see Davey engaged in a rhythmic battle of vibrations and echoes which were stemming from a pair of Dr. Dre's beats headphones. For kicks, I took a stab at guessing which songs he was listening to by studying his movements and mimicking his lip syncs. True to form, Davey set out to shock the world with his eccentric ensemble, which he later told me was inspired by the legendary *Afrika Bambaataa*. From the grey cat fur in his earring down to the magnetic clasp on a multi-colored cummerbund, our eclectic choreographer was destined to be an everlasting memory in an event that was billed to be unforgettable.

Gus fiddled around with his old black and grey Casio wrist watch. The CA-90 with the push button numbers on the face was definitely antique-, but he kept it clean and found a way to have his alarm play the song that Mr. Softee uses on his ice cream trucks. Using his right thumb and forefinger to brace its squared face whilst twisting his left forearm counterclockwise every ten minutes reaffirmed what experience had taught me time and time again. Gus was growing increasingly agitated at waiting for an invisible chauffeur, and Calvin's repeated inability to produce something that didn't require a plan B meant that it was only a matter of time before he reached his capacity and unleashed a barrage of un-pleasantries in his direction.

"Here we go again! All dressed up with somewhere to go, but no way to get there. Thanks again Mr. Budget Rent-A-Car. I can't call you an Enterprise because unlike you, they do pick people up!" shouted Gus.

"He's coming, bro! Take it easy and play with your Sesame Street preschool watch with the Count Von Count keypad," replied Calvin.

Everyone turned their heads in Calvin's direction, as it was the first time we have ever heard a reply like that from him.

"Oh, that was a good one Cal. Who pulled your puppet strings on that one? That couldn't have come from you, because if it did, it would have bombed like every other idea you've ever had. The only ideas you don't get are the ones that actually work" said Gus.

"Chill, fellas. Don't destroy the night - I'll call a cab," said Izzy.

He reached inside his jacket and pulled out his cell phone, but before he could type in the numbers, he received an incoming call from his mother. As he answered and began conversing almost immediately, a slew of horizontally-challenged wrinkles exploded upon his forehead. From years of experience I could decipher that look and its awful origin - his mom was somewhere hanging out with Uncle Al. He said a few words to her, then ended the call with, "I love you and I'll see you later." He raised his head and we made eye contact; his eyes told me everything without his mouth saying a word. I just shook my head and tried to negate the infusion of depressive self-commiseration by nodding my head in the direction of Davey, who was oblivious to all that was occurring outside of his musical sanctum.

"There are times when I sincerely envy Davey. I sure wish I could open that door and play in his world upon the feeling of spontaneity" said Izzy.

I countered with an upheaved request of inclusion. *"Guys, you know what would be great?"*

The perked-up tone of my voice and animated facial expression summoned the pupils of all who were present in the room. Davey slid from under his headphones and awaited my continuance.

"We should hop on the train. It would be like old times, plus it would put us right in front of the venue."

"The train?" said Calvin. *"Why would we get all dressed up with somewhere to go and then choose the most hideous way to get there? I don't know about taking the subway being dressed like an oblong penguin. Somehow, it just screams vulnerability to all the dangers lying in wait for some indigenous throwbacks such as ourselves."*

"We'd be more like a bunch of drenched Dalmatians if we go out in this weather" chimed Gus. *"The very last thing we should do right now is panic and abandon Calvin's idea of grandiose travel and earth-shattering entrance into the party. We've waited this long; we may as well stick with the original plan."*

"Gus, a minute ago you were ridiculing Calvin for his idea, now you're co-signing the plan? At least two-face used a coin to help him flip flop on an idea."

"I'm in!" says Davey.

"Me too!" yelled Izzy.

Gus rolled his eyes around the room as if to ignore the increasing popularity of a mechanical trip down memory lane. He bent his left elbow ninety degrees and punched in some numerical code using the keypad of his Enterprise Spock watch. We stood in intrigued silence as "the old Jamaican Candy-Man" took his time and methodically mashed on the rubber oval buttons, then paused to look at the faded digital screen.

"Gus!" yelled Calvin. "What are you doing?"

Gus sucked his pearly white teeth and replied "Hold on. I'm trying to text message my friend to let her know of the change in plans and that we won't be arriving together. Does anyone know if they are checking for Identification at the door?"

Simultaneously, we all fell off our seats and let out a sigh that not only confirmed Gus' identity as that guy you don't bring home to meet daddy, but it also signaled the end of the transportation debate. One by one, we exited Izzy's condo and jigsaw puzzled ourselves into the elevator headed for the lobby. The buttons illuminated themselves around each numerical landing plateau as we descended from the hovering heights of the city skyline down towards the sinister streets of lower Manhattan. As the doors retracted themselves, unveiling the new scene we had been dropped into, I saw the doorman standing near the revolving door with his right hand held high above his shoulder. He smiled at us as if he was watching his favorite blue-and-orange team emerge from the dark garden tunnel and prepare for battle with the opposing team. His broad smile tickled the silly kid in me as I envisioned how his missing chicklets gave the appearance of a nicely-dressed dental experiment gone wrong. I dropped my head slightly and belly-chuckled in-between our neatly choreographed exit routine. With the cry of winds just on the other side of the heavy swivel door, we each high-fived our number-one fan, then barreled our way approximately one hundred and eighty degrees into the dark, drenched night.

Wearing stoic expressions, we made our way through the torrential downpour of rain that continuously rode invisible sequences of descending air pockets, creating a distorted vision of a sideways slide of every object just outside of an arm's length. Along the way, our shiny shoes dove head first into puddles of water which dispersed upon impact, and quickly reassembled themselves like indestructible amoebas of liquid. Upon the deepest submergence of my left foot, I felt the shock overtake my ankle and make its way up the calf muscle of my leg. Instinctively, I jiggled my foot to shake free of the excess liquid, but like a soldier facing extreme life circumstances, I stayed the course and never broke stride.

We reached the warm shelter of the subway system with anticipated delight. The steel grates below our feet allowed the familiar smells of an underground passageway to seep between the hairs within our nostrils, massaging our memories back into a time when sixty-five cents or a brass coin with the carved out initials *N.Y.C.* would pay for an unlimited one-way ride across four of the five boroughs. Like a group of adolescent kids who'd stumbled upon a bag of lost favorite toys, we began enjoying all the subtle nuances and hidden dangers that are infused within the DNA of a native New Yorker.

"Remember when the Guardian Angels used to patrol the cars and platforms with their red painter's caps? Ed Koch thought they were 'thugs', but people loved seeing them during the late night hours," said Gus.

"Yeah, I remember them. Curtis sure had those boys fighting crime with their bare hands," Izzy recalled.

"Remember the dirty old men who only rode the crowded areas of the train to ride up on the girls who couldn't find a seat?" Calvin reminded us.

"Who? Gus?" Izzy blurted out.

We all laughed until the breath in our lungs had made its exit and was preparing to re-enter the cycle of oxygen that generally kept us alive. Davey held tightly onto his headphones while leaning over the yellow line to look down the dark tunnel, hoping for the shimmer of white light to shrink his pupils.

"Do y'all remember the deaf dudes that used to come through and put the cards on your lap explaining how they were hearing impaired and asking for donations?" asked Izzy, "They used to put you on the spot to donate. You didn't want to say no in front of all the other riders."

"Well, I used to call out to them in a low tone once they got past me and if they turned around, I ripped up my card and gave them back my plastic flower," Gus mused.

I looked up and saw Davey jumping down onto the tracks. It scared me so that I screamed his name, startling everyone and making them turn in the direction where Davey had once stood. Moments later, a single hand appeared onto the platform, followed by its twin clutching a pair of red headphones.

"What the hell are you doing, Davey?"

"I dropped my headphones. At two hundred and fifty dollars a pop, I wasn't about to leave 'em".

"Dude, your life is worth more than two-fifty!"

We shook our heads and tried to calm our hearts from the momentary mindless behavior displayed by Davey, but he was such a calm soul and so entrenched in his musical sanctum that it made no sense to continuously harp on anything that negated a harmonious flow. The rest of us went back to searching our minds for other underground memories to recall. One by one, forgotten occurrences from our past began to roll off our tongues, which made us laugh until we heard the rumblings and felt the vibrations of a fast-approaching subway car.

Protruding from the darkness of the colossal cave came this massive metal contraption, which barreled its way into the lighted station, providing momentary glimpses of its internal makeup with every passing window. Once the electrical behemoth had come to a halt, we moved in for a closer look and discovered that she had been through much more turmoil than we had that night. Spray-painted across her torso was the notification that

"Charlie Wuz Here" and that *"Mike double hearts Tanya"*. I remember sarcastically thinking to myself that Tanya is really a lucky girl and that Charlie must have had a schedule conflict; why else would he decide to leave a message?

The double sliding doors opened and we entered the belly of the beast simultaneously, while the previous a la carte items were being regurgitated. We took seats similar to the ones we would place our hind sides in during our return from a disheartened night at Madison Square Garden.

"See, I told y'all that it wasn't gonna be that bad. In a few minutes, we will be having the time of our lives. Mark my words, tonight will be unforgettable!"

I could see that my words were injecting excitement back into the group. Calvin decided to pump up the volume a bit by making us aware of a huge surprise he had in store for the guest of honor. Izzy was visibly delighted and we all made a big deal out of what lay ahead. Just like old times, our joyous band of brothers was once again in tune with each other and reminiscent of a time within our past; Davey stood up and put on a display of dancing that was nothing short of mesmerizing. Soon, we had the entire subway car engaged in an impromptu jam session.

We traveled our route from bright station to dark tunnel then back again, and mingled with the other passengers as if we had scripted a prelude to the party. I kept a roving eye on the names of the scheduled stops so that we would not miss our destination. During my peripheral scour, I couldn't help but notice this one young woman who seemed completely overzealous with Davey and his unique be-bop swagger. She cornered herself with him immediately and after a few words, I could see Davey putting his headphones over her ears. She smiled at him and began a suggestive dance sequence of her own and before you could blink, the two were in a full-fledged dance battle.

Over the loud speaker, we could hear the conductor announce the approaching station and I began to gather the troops. Like we had done nine stations prior, our metal car screeched into the lighted terminal, opened the sliding doors, exchanged a few passengers and prepared to depart and repeat - but just as the doors were about to shut, the jovial young woman took off running with Davey's headset. Utilizing cat-like reflexes, he was able to dart out behind her before the doors collided together, rendering the rest of us totally helpless and he extremely vulnerable. From an incapable position, we pressed our faces against the thick Plexiglas windows of the train, hoping that the doors would once again free themselves and allow us the opportunity to reunite. Suddenly, the train began to pull away from the lighted station and our desperate eyes continued to look outwards, hoping to ultimately catch a glimpse of Davey attached to his headphones and embracing a triumphant smile.

Izzy frantically pulled out his cell phone to try and dial 9-1-1, but in this dungeonous underworld, sandwiched between Earth's core and the illumination of the nocturnal city lights, a cellular signal is all but non-existent. Moments later, two loud firecracker pops and a heart wrenching scream rang out from an invisible entity hiding within the station. With the subway car moving at a rate just above a slow jog and increasing steadily, our oversized rectangular peepholes allowed us to view the roving imperfections within the tiled walls and concrete floor, followed by a trail of abandoned trash, a group of onlookers chaotically huddled over a large object and then finally, we faded to black.

CHAPTER 18:
THE CLEANSING

"Would anyone care to come to the front and say a few words?" asked the pastor.

We all looked at each other, then all eyes focused their attention towards Izzy. From years of experience, everyone had learnt to use him as a barometer for gauging the level of functionality within our tight-knit group. The long, awkward period of silence danced throughout the large room with white vaulted ceilings and multicolored artwork on the windows. It crept up in between our legs and pinched us all in the backside, forcing us all to stand up simultaneously.

"We do!" shouted Izzy.

Immediately, we became the focus of all in attendance. As we maneuvered towards the front of the room, I could tell that Izzy's heart was heavy, still dealing with the anxiety of stage fright from his last speaking engagement. I couldn't help but think that somewhere up there, where the angels play, Davey was cheering us on and routing for his good friend to conquer a formidable foe that had now taken residency within his mind.

We stood behind Izzy as he approached the podium. Underneath his eyelids were the signage of sorrow which continued to pool after every blink and attempt an escape from the tips of his long, curved eyelashes. Understanding the emotions that were mingling within the audience, Izzy gathered himself together and stood erect to address them by telling a story of which even I had been unaware.

"*Every minute of every day is calibrated by the additions and extractions that GOD makes within our kingdom of life. A majestic balance that only HE can control is sometimes viewed as inhumane, harsh and unforgiving because of deep emotional attachments. But the cycle of life is a wonderful journey that each of us must go through and unfortunately, sometimes the journey is interrupted by ungodly bullshit. Today, we are gathered here as a representation of expression, constipated by sullen grief and intangible denial because one of our loved ones has met a horrific fate and lost his life over some bullshit. One of my best friends and emotional mentors is no longer here to show us how to excite joy and organic passion within our own lives and it sickens my soul, because he was more than deserving of all the beauty and joy that comes with a long life. David was a phenomenon. Deep down, I believe he knew it and he wasn't afraid to be himself in the face of ignorance. He was a leader in the charge for inner peace and self-esteem minus the egocentricity. He was forever radiant when engaged in creation, but it overflowed whenever he danced. It was this space in time that made me marvel at what Davey could do. His genius taught me to focus on my own internal conflicts and to right the wrongs that dwell from within before they completely rob you of joy. It took me a while to understand this concept, but it all came to a head one afternoon when we were teens. See, there was this dance tournament that Davey was unsure of because of all the participation from rivaled competition. He desperately wanted to be a part of this event, but was up to his ears in anxiety because he had never shown his stuff in a public forum. His nervous energy forced him to dig deep and soul search until he bottomed out and faced his truth. And that TRUTH became the tagline for his life: ANSWER ONLY TO THE VOICE FROM WITHIN. Well, needless to say, Davey chose to follow his passion from that day forth and began separating himself as the most creative dancer out of the pack. During day three of the four-day competition, one of the other contestants turned to the instructor and said, "Wow! DAVID IS PUTTING US TO SHAME!"*

Everyone smiled and applauded the heartfelt tale Izzy shared about our beloved friend. I stood back for a moment and squinted my left eye as I internalized the final words from Izzy's tale. There was something about them that felt familiar to me, like I had heard them before, and the inability to pin down their origin was definitely going to cause me some anxiety until I figured it out.

Over my right shoulder, I could see the tears streaming down the face of my headstrong Jamaican brother. He was always the most vocal about Davey and his propensity to gyrate anywhere and at any time. Deep down, I knew he embraced him and I could only imagine the sorrow that was hiding amongst the drag of his drooping jowls and the immense guilt that was hovering over his heart. Calvin woefully sobbed on my left shoulder until his eyes were filled with protrusions of tiny blood vessels that noticeably lined his pupils. At that particular moment, I was absolutely certain that there were no thoughts of capitalism nor entrepreneurship rolling around in that abnormal head of his.

Under my breath and in-between the sniffles, I spoke a few heartfelt words into the universe, where I figured Davey was, and prayed for his spirit. Beneath heavy, tear-laden lids, my eyes danced an epic soliloquy of grace while my brain repeatedly displayed images of happier times upon a jet-black screen. I could feel a fragmented force sweep across my torso and momentarily arrest my gentle back and forth sway. My wet face briefly garnered a smile. We motored back to our seated positions in the audience and awaited the conclusion of the sermon. It felt so surreal that our life-long group would forever be physically diminished by one.

Upon exiting the building, Izzy and I decided to go in an opposite direction from the rest of the devastated mourners. Aware that his pace was a tad faster, I quickened my pick-ups and put-downs until we were walking in unison. Traveling southwest on Columbus Avenue only to make a left onto Broadway, we passed the Metropolitan Opera and the back side of the Trump Hotel before coming to a halt on a bench in Columbus Circle. I stood there intrigued by the question of why we were standing in midtown, where the tranquility of Central Park ends and the majesty of Manhattan begins. Izzy turned over his right shoulder and stared long and hard at the First Republic Bank and all of the surrounding shops in the circle. A few minutes later, he turned over his left shoulder and buried himself within the concrete-squared circles that led into the park.

The Goliath nature of Central Park aroused Izzy's thoughts of becoming a little David and losing himself within the welcoming sways of the trees. Visions of people sitting on the green grass, horse and carriage rides, rollerblading pairs and energized two-year-olds being chased by their parents opened the part of his mind that was directly affixed to his heart.

"THIS is what life is about!" he wailed. *"See those children there? I guarantee you that they have no idea what menacing forces are just outside the walls of this temporary afternoon community."*

"Of course they don't! They are only children," I replied with a sprinkle of sarcasm.

"You're missing the whole point, my friend. The obliviousness I am speaking to is the soil in which the seeds of dreams are planted. Fear, doubt and circumstance are the diseased elements that this type of community is

inoculated against. This section of manicured city life is a direct contrast to the story that is told just beyond those stone dividers. In here, I am reminded to exhale long enough to empty the toxins from my lungs then slowly inhale a much-needed breath of fresh air."

I shook my head up and down to let him know that I understood where he was coming from and where he wanted to go. Although I was thinking he was being a bit dramatic, I realized that we had just come from saying farewell to one of our best friends and his heart may have been heavy and weighing on his emotional state. Faintly, we heard a sound similar to a distant static, which forced us to align our eyes above the trees and witness a plane appear then disappear amongst the skyline and the multiple bales of white clouds. With us stuck in a freeze-frame, from behind I'm sure we resembled two pound puppies fascinated by an unobtainable moving object due to the way we both tilted our heads to the same side. I have seen many planes fly above the skyscrapers and disappear into the clouds, but this one was different. I could see that this one was carrying the soul and spirit of a passenger who never made it to the departure gate. Once the aircraft divorced our natural vision, I felt its allure engage Izzy's desires and culminate with his fatigued whisper of the words "I'm done!" I was uncertain of what he meant with the low utterance of that phrase, but tried to lighten the load with smiles and jokes as we resumed our trek down

8th avenue, soaking in sights and triggering forgotten memories of a time when life was more about beginnings than endings.

Before there was ever a Fantastic Four, there was the Awesome Two - Izzy and I, and this felt like old times. Heightened by a level of sensitivity brought on by grief, we became emotionally involved with the multitude of memories that came pouring in with each sidewalk we stepped onto and left behind. The complex nature in which our emotions chose to release themselves spoke volumes to the pain burrowed deep within our chests. We traced 8th avenue with our footsteps and role-played, using characters from our past, in every large-mirrored window we passed along the way. In a weird kind of way, it became our way to harness our dark horse and deal with the anguish.

Coupled with every character change came the shifting of an insatiable sorrow. The reflective images displayed within the frames of each passing window told their own story and with the help of condensation, cried their own set of tears. Our ever-changing mobile audience found themselves privy to small parts of our roving life-play as it continued down the avenue, evoking crunchy facial expressions and matador dance steps from other pedestrians, all the way to the marquee housed in front of Madison Square Garden.

We stopped.

We looked.

We laughed.

Once again, grief had brought us to a familiar place; a place so grand that it would dwarf any circumstance that interfered with the creation of our smiles. It was an unforgettable blanketing place, whose history was woven so deep within our DNA that we felt as though this was our home away from home.

Izzy and I began walking up the steps towards the entrance, both of us trying to wipe away the dried white streaks that began at the base of our eyelids and stretched just beyond our cheekbones. Neither of us spoke a word. Our hearts just took over and led us inside. We stood frozen just inside the invisible doors as if we were waiting for Patrick Ewing to come show us around. There was no mistaking the fact that this place lifted our spirits and reversed our frowns. Ironically, we both shut our eyes at the same time so that we could see into the past when we would wear our Knick uniforms here and test the competence of court security. In remembrance of our friend, we both decided to engage into a goofy wiggle and an exaggerated jiggle that allowed his spirit to once again meander the halls and become the new miracle on 34th street.

"Israel! Israel Lemhi!" shouted a familiar voice.

The vocal jolt catapulted us back to the present and when we were able to focus on its origin, we were surprised to find Calvin's new business associate, Mr. Pennar, staring directly at us. He extended his hand to embrace ours then expressed his condolences for the loss of our buddy. Dressed in the same M.I.B. suit that Will Smith wore when he saved Orion from the bugs, Mr. Pennar tried to take our minds away from the pain temporarily by inviting us to his new office.

"You have an office in here?" asked Izzy.

"Yes! I just got set up today" he explained. *"Come, take a walk with me. We are testing a new fragrance and its reaction to different body types. It would be great to have you try it and to get your honest feedback."*

We followed behind him like two kids in a candy store. There we were, inside the world's most famous arena, where our buddy had finally made a connection with someone who was really making it happen. I couldn't be more proud of Calvin at that very moment. We made a left turn and headed up escalators and onto the Mezzanine floor. I pulled out my phone to call Triple C and let him know that we were we were about to have the M.O.P. experience firsthand and to congratulate his persistence throughout all of the all of the ridicule. I held my phone up as we continued to follow Morris Pennar down another corridor heading towards some

heading towards some executive offices. My cellular signal was weak inside

the building, so my call got stuck in dial mode until we could enter an area

where the connection could occur. Morris then makes a sharp right turn

into the men's room. We stood outside the restroom entrance, awaiting his

return. He stuck his arm out and motioned for us to follow him, but we

were a bit apprehensive. Neither of us had the need to use the facilities at

that moment, so we politely declined his offer.

"Come on, guys! Step into my office!" he urged.

"THIS IS YOUR OFFICE?" we replied.

"Yes! Please go over to the sink and wash your hands."

"Wait a minute... What the heck is this?" asked Izzy.

*"THIS is **M.O.P.** fragrances. This is my **M**ist **O**ver **P**iss operation."*

We both stood stunned at what we had just witnessed. Shocked

and confused, I looked at Izzy and he was walking over towards the sink. He

washed his hands thoroughly then allowed Morris to spray one of his

fragrances onto his wrists. Raising his hands just under his nose, Izzy took a

whiff of the product and smiled at Morris, giving him nonverbal approval.

We left the lavatory with a sense of urgency. We dashed down the stairwell

and emerged from the shadows through the heavy invisible doors. Once we touched the blacktop of 8th avenue, we laughed hysterically until our bellies were painful, and our breath elusive.

In-between our raucous cackling and snotty nose snippets, my cellular phone signal increased and unknowingly connected to complete the call to Calvin.

"Hello? Hello? Hello?

Unfortunately, our uncontrollable laughter did not allow us to respond. All we knew was that the Garden was in good hands with Morris and Calvin. Yep - clean, scent-y hands!

CHAPTER 19:
WHAT DOES IT ALL MEAN

"I got it!"

I opened my eyes with a manic fervor. It was 3:15am and my mind had finally solved the riddle that was stifling its functionality for weeks. During the funeral, when Izzy had uttered, **"Davey Is Putting Us To Shame"**, it triggered something in me as I felt an uncanny familiarity to its narration.

D.I.P.U.T.S.

It's the exact same phrase he created to repeatedly take revenge on Harland. And throughout the years, it had been utilized masterfully on numerous occasions to display emotions. Izzy once told me that he was repeatedly referred to in a manner so unfitting to his true self that his self-esteem took a beating. He said the verbal onslaught he endured would rip through the fibers of his soul like a parasite, and even to that day, it continued to poke at his psyche. When looking for this apathetic individual in the mirror, all that was staring back at him would be someone totally different. He knew his reflection displayed an inner strength capable of dreaming the inevitable and achieving the impossible. He never did divulge the actual word used by a certain leather coat and matching hat wearer, but it all made sense now; it was all coming into focus.

Lifting my head away from the indentations formed within my memory foam pillow, I continued to replay past conversations of Izzy and I and some of the interesting things he would share with me about his life behind that heavy metal door. I knew that the physical and mental abuse that he went through as a kid took more of a toll on him than he would care to admit, and this is what fueled his repeated actions to *right a wrong* with such passion and emotion. When I thought about the things that made him happy, it was not surprising that they were a direct contrast to life as we knew it growing up. The peaceful surroundings, the powerful positive affirmations, the need to fly just underneath the radar and not be singled out are all contrary to a previous life that festered amongst a heavily-charged minefield and demanded the purple heart of a committed soldier.

Hours later, I found myself inexplicably standing on the banks of the East River, skipping rocks and enjoying some time and space. Sifting through the colorful rock piles and discarding the big bulky kinds that would clunk and sink towards the bottom, I sought out the lightweight oval stones that laid nicely in-between my thumb and forefinger. One after another, I watched in amazement as the perfectly-thrown stones kissed the surface of the water then, surfed amongst the juvenile white tips of the waves. The black dirt on my hands felt good while the thin air surrounding my body impregnated my lungs, gently brushed across my face and whistled a tune just outside my eardrums. My teeth were cold from smiling and the palpitations from my heart spelled out joy in Morse code. I had never found this to be amusing to me as a kid, but for some odd reason, I was simply just enjoying this alone time with myself.

I stood along the river for hours, just allowing myself to be free and enjoy a fee-less pleasure that was always at my disposal, but always viewed as a huge no-no for my image. Back in the days, if there was ever a rock in my hand, it would be hurled at an object with the intent to cause damage - because in our neighborhood, it was how we excited the crowd and cquired respect amongst our peers. The more outrageous the act, the more excitement attached to your image, resulting in the inflation of your desired street cred. But my mind was so removed from that line of thought that it was painstaking to recall that memory right then. I can understand now why Izzy felt the need to reverse his curse. I could feel his need to breathe. Startled by the bombastic nature of my ringtone, the zenful room with the river view that comprised my inner sanctum came crashing down around me as if someone had hurled a rock inside.

Reluctantly, I answered the phone.

"Hello!"

"What, you too good to call anybody?" replied the caller.

"Who is this?" I asked. The demonic voice on the other end of the line seemed to be wrestling with a bout of possession. I could not tell if it

was a male or female on the line for the first few seconds, until I figured out who the mystery person was.

"...be there soon!" I hung up the phone and summoned Izzy.

"Yeah, I already know" he said. "Seems like my favorite uncle showed up bearing gifts again. I'm heading there now."

Once again, Izzy swooped in to save the day - to right a wrong; to reverse a curse. Under my breath, I bid a sorrowed farewell to my new-found activity and all the pleasantries that came along with It. My attitude began its slow metamorphosis to become what was necessary to function in the presence of unpredictable chaos and extreme anguish. Before the call, my head was lifted high in the clouds; now, I was fixated on the imperfections of the ground, gearing up to deal with an exorcism. It all happened so fast that I thought my head had twisted around.

I knew some hard decisions had to be made. The time had come where we had to do something drastic, as we were becoming prisoners of a translucent genie in a bottle. I didn't know which words I would use when I spoke to Izzy, but this reverse guardianship had to stop and I had to get him to see the big picture. The reality was that our lives had become a string of movie scenes shot in high definition 1080p. With makeshift villains, damsels in distress, knights in shining armor, invisible bullies, probable cause and definitive effects, we had all the necessary ingredients for a lifetime of drama.

Standing on the subway platform, listening to the roar from the incoming and outgoing trains caused me to shed a tear. I knew Davey's spirit was with me and I needed him to help me carry out my mission. I mouthed a thank you into the universe, as I wanted him to know that I acknowledged his presence and I smiled when, from across the tracks, a street dancer performing on a distorted piece of brown cardboard, looked me in the eyes and nodded his head up and down. I was so moved, that I walked to the other side of the station platform to where he was performing, reached into my pocket and placed one hundred dollars in his tarnished tin cup. His thankful eyes solidified all that I had felt and needed to know, and before I left something, propelled me to whisper to him:

"...*D*ancers *I*nfluence *P*eople *U*nlike *T*oucan *S*am!"

"What?"

He looked at me with a bewildered stare as I realized my use of the D.I.P.U.T.S. acronym was not as prolific as Izzy's. I turned and walked away from the man as if I had just enlightened him with some newfound truth. All the while, I was embarrassed to say the least, and I picked up my pace in an attempt to disappear into the darkness at the top of the staircase and reappear far away on the other side of the platform. I could hear Davey chuckling at me uncontrollably and I figured that once I got onto the subway car, he would go back and give an explanation to his protégé.

I arrived at my destination not knowing what to expect. Stepping through the heavy metal door always brought back vivid memories of a time when two young minds were susceptible to the gnarly grip and grueling teachings of a way of life unbeknownst to the masses. I had to prepare myself to become the emotional support my best friend needed. I inhaled two large, deep breaths and placed my right hand on the doorknob. Tightening my grip in preparation for a clockwise turn of the silver sphere, the door flew open and I stumbled forward. Standing firm on the other side of the shiny threshold was Izzy. Drenched in anxiety and speculation, he turned swiftly and led me up the rusty box steel staircase and into the claustrophobic elevator that reeked of urine and feces. Within his eyes, all I could see was my own reflection. It was one of the few times that I could not open the tinted windows to his soul. I felt like an accomplice to a pre-crime that I had no idea had occurred. Somewhere within that confined mechanical lift space was a silent cry for help. The question soon became whose cry it was.

Upon entering the apartment, it was quickly concluded that we were late to the party and missed all of the festive nuances. Staring at us through 1.75 liters of thick distorted glass, Uncle Al donned a devilish smirk while rocking back and forth in his seat, seemingly content with the turmoil he had created. Izzy's mom, clearly dealing with the inebriated aftermath of her incestuous dealings with Uncle Al, laid slumped over in a seat at the front table. Her cognitive functions were clearly in need of a lifeline and the increasing conflict between her irises and pupils kept my hands hovering over the digital keypad, ready to dial 9-1-1. I was swimming in an array of incomprehensive emotions and could only imagine what thoughts were permeating Izzy's head. I knew for a fact that his heart was crushed; I could feel it, but his inner strength was on duty and preparing to work overtime.

I extended my right arm and placed it around the shoulders of my best friend. He was in need of a sturdy place to lean, and I was the one he was most familiar with. Seemingly stuck in a state of shock, he stood steadfast with his head held high and his vision lurking past the present and further down the narrow corridor of the apartment. Burrowing in through one of the windows from the back bedrooms, crept the remnants of dwindling sunlight which paraded off of some foreign object, casting a distorted shadow of intense intrigue and bone-chilling suspense. Someone, it seemed, was hiding just beyond the curvature of the wall and out of plain sight. I watched in amazement as the grown man standing next to me a moment ago slowly began answering the beckoning call of this opaque enigma. He stretched his arms out to the width of the walls and walked towards the back of the apartment. With each soft step he took, I could see the emergence of the frightened little boy who once upon a time buried his cries within the frilly patterns of these faded wall coverings.

Armed with the belief of a shifting persona who had undoubtedly recognized the distorted outline of this faceless image, and yielding a shiny, jagged-edged survival tool that seemed to appear from thin air, my best friend was poised to deliver justice for the little boy and his abducted innocence. The infusion of heightened emotion and distant memories oozing from behind the failing adhesive strips jolted themselves into his aura. The muscles within his forearms became tense. The grip supplied to the handle of his weapon was suffocating. Finally, this was his moment to right a wrong; this was the opportunity for which he had waited so long. Slowly, he positioned his back flat against the wall just short of the curvature. I could see his mouth moving, but could not figure out what was being uttered.

Was he counting to ten?

Could it be that he was listening to my voice and taking direction to pause, then breathe?

My answers would soon appear as I witnessed the repeated inflation and deflation within his facial composition, marrying his likeness to that of jazz legend Dizzy Gillespie minus the eccentric instrument.

To no avail, I feverously flapped my arms and shook my head from left to right. Standing just outside the corridor, prophetically miming the word *'NO'* was the only defense at my disposal. My sole intent was to distract this non-combative soldier gone awry and have him abort his coveted mission, but compressed anger exacerbated old wounds and excreted violence from beneath the scabbing. Fueled with immense anticipation and intense hostility, Izzy turned the corner, faced his perceived enemy and swung his survival tool with incapacitating force and earth-shattering intent. The blow struck its intended target perfectly, separating a torso from its infrastructure.

"Whew! Your mom's dress form!" I said with a relief.

Izzy stood motionless. Surveying the aftermath with a scowl and frustrated that his intended target had once again eluded his wrath, he gathered the felonious instrument from the grips of the tan rug fibers and exited the apartment. I quietly followed behind him - close enough to be confused with his shadow and equally perturbed by what had just occurred. Fortunately for everyone, there was no blood spilled nor any crime scene to be investigated. There was no need for authorities to be summoned or witness statements to be obtained. Vengeance had suffered a loss that evening and did not have the ability to remain in an anger-less environment, so with its thick green tail tucked between two weary hind legs, it managed to finagle itself in-between our choreographed footsteps and headed for the elevator. As the view of the apartment began to vanish, I felt something reach way down into my front pocket, clutch the final flat oval stone and hurl it towards the evil genie in the bottle.

CHAPTER 20:
Peace, Prosperity and the Unfathomable Unicorn

The taxicab ride back into our perceived reality ironically depicted images of our rights of passage. Encapsulated within the black plastic barrier of the vehicle's rearview mirror were the infamous red and white pillars of the Con Edison energy plant. Traveling in an opposite direction and having the billows of smoke behind us was a representation of the hard work and determination we had put in to give ourselves a fighting chance to reach the other side of the rainbow. Contrarily, the panoramic views of the majestic Manhattan skyline, surrounded by a picture perfect sunset, granted us access into a world of sophistication, success and endless possibilities.

"Sir, would you please pull over and stop the car?" Izzy directed.

Looking totally puzzled and confused, the driver responded, *"Where? Here?"*

"Yessir! Right here, right now."

The driver pulled alongside the service ramp of the bridge and put the car into park. Izzy opened his door and dashed across three lanes of traffic, looked over his left shoulder and motioned for me to follow, jumped over the median and dodged three additional lanes of oncoming cars, only to come to a halt at a familiar place of reminisce.

"Remember this view?"

"Yes I do," I answered.

"Tell me what you see?"

I looked at him with a puzzling stare.

"C'mon man, tell me what you see."

"Um... I see tall buildings; I see traffic - oh, and I still smell the stench from the river below."

"What's missing?" he asked.

I shrugged my shoulders, crumpled my face and mimed my feelings of confusion.

"CHANGE!" he shouted. *"It's the one thing humans hate most. Some changes are huge - like the new skyline that frames lower Manhattan and some are as subtle as viewing things from a different angle. I've stood here and adjusted my lenses a few times in an attempt to escape mediocrity, but unfortunately, when the fog is wiped away, the views become familiar. I always felt that life began on the other side of this steel gray rainbow, but what I now know is that for me, there is another jump."*

Immediately, I became flushed with fear. My mind raced into a warped thought pattern of repeated fatal actions and suicidal propensity.

The speed with which my heart was beating increased exponentially. Instinct drove me to reach out and secure both of his wrists while staring directly into his eyes,

"If you choose to end it right here and now, then you choose to end it for the both of us!"

My bluff was stern and as believable as the official story of September 11th. I sincerely did not want to put a halt to my existence and I was betting that he would not make that determination for me. He matched my stare and asked,

"What are you doing? I was not thinking about jumping from this bridge dude! I was talking about MOVING!"

"Huh?"

"YES! Moving away!"

"Oh, I apologize. Please forgive me for shackling you down."

"I'm ok, buddy. It's cool and very refreshing to see how much you care, my friend. By the way, you may need to do something about those fingernails. My wrists now look like two murder victims."

We both laughed all the way back to our cab, across the bridge and into the late evening. Each moment of laughter spawned the memory of another, but I knew that change he spoke about was soon to materialize and the reality I faced was either jump ship or climb aboard for the ride.

The following day, Izzy received a call from Kathleen, inviting him to dinner as she was in town for a few days. Micro had expanded his business into specialized diabetic care and scheduled Kathleen to transport a new patient to receive Dialysis treatment at New York Hospital. This was her first trip into the city without Micro, and the sight of a familiar face would be invaluable. He agreed to meet with her and even suggested a meeting place within close proximity of the hospital, so that she would not spend time fighting the rush-hour traffic.

I watched him as he meticulously prepared himself to meet Kathleen. Back and forth he went throughout the place, combing and re-combing his hair, double-checking his attire and making an appearance in every mirror that would accept him. Before he left, he turned to me and said,

"Life is what you make it - and I am back to being creative."

I couldn't help but imagine if there was more to this meeting than that of two old friends catching up. Nah, I knew Izzy too well, and if there was some hidden agenda, I would have been the first to know about it.

I went to the mirror and marveled at my own reflection. I took a few careful moments to examine my being. Some had said that I was Izzy's carbon copy and yes, we did have similar features, but I was taller than he was with his shoes off, and my skin complexion was caramel whilst his was more of a creamed coffee. We both dealt with issues of trust and sharing our thoughts with others, but he was more of the calculated, thought provoking type. I lived in the moment and worried about things when they arose. My motto had always been that if things weren't broken, don't try and repair them. If there was a knock at the door, I would address it once I knew they really wanted to enter. It may have just be a case of a wrong address.

I always believed that Izzy was locked in a constant battle of being true to himself and actually knowing what that truth really was. I had a clear picture of WHO I was and WHY I was. I was nosy and inquisitive because my grandmother was nosy and inquisitive. She gave a new meaning to the term *neighborhood watch* and I inherited it through her gene pool. So standing in front of this mirror having a conversation with myself was not as interesting as finding out what Izzy had up his sleeve. Come to think of it, my stomach was grumbling and I needed to get some food. I pondered where I should go for a minute, before heading off.

I arrived just in time for dinner to be served and decided to forgo any appetizer and salad bowl. My carnivorous appetite was approaching the red warning levels on the hunger scale and it did not make any sense to be teased with a sip of hot water and a bowl of tossed grass leaves. Thankfully, Izzy had already ordered for us and this nice succulent sirloin was exactly what I needed to cure my ailment. I sat quietly and ate my dinner as the two of them strolled back down memory lane, crossed the streets of years past and returned via reminisce road.

Kathleen kept a watchful eye on her smartphone as she did not want to miss the call from the hospital notifying her that her patient's dialysis treatment had been completed. She said he was scheduled to have 4 initial treatments at the hospital and then be redirected to have services rendered within the local facility. The process was underway to match him with a successful kidney donor, but he had other internal issues that she did not care to mention as if the HIPPA police was eavesdropping at our table.

"By the way, I wanted to ask you a huge favor."

"Sure!" she replied, "What is it?"

"Well, remember my friend I told you about a long time ago...?"

"You mean the one who lived with the leather-coat man?"

"Yes, that's him. Well, he wants to find his biological father and has his social security number. I was wondering if you would be able to input the information into the medical insurance database and give him an address."

"Israel, I cannot do that. That is illegal."

"I understand Kathleen, and I feel ashamed for asking, but I felt this would be the most accurate way to locate him. It's been rumored that he had cancer and my friend needs to know if his father is dead or alive."

"Cancer? Wow, I'm sorry. Ok, I'll do it this time but never again. Keep this just between you and me as I can get into big trouble. I have my laptop in the van. I can logon from there."

From the corners of my half-moon smile, I gently wiped away the excess A-1 sauce. I nodded to myself as it was becoming clear to me what Izzy's intentions were. He was attempting to confront his tormentor and I must say, persuading Kathleen to utilize her resources was nothing short of genius. I followed behind them, not saying a word. Maybe this was fate. Maybe this was his destiny. Time is supposed to heal all wounds, but just maybe some wounds are too infected to heal on their own.

We exited the restaurant single-file. Izzy was first, I was last and Kathleen was shielded in-between. Izzy pushed open the large front door enough for Kathleen to walk through and I scurried to beat the closure as I found it a little weird that she allowed the door to swing back, almost slamming into my face. Could it be that she was irritated I had shown up? I didn't make a fuss about it. Maybe she still had some sauce on her fingers and the door slid away from her grasp. I chose to focus on the positive and up ahead about two hundred paces was a convenience store that was being guarded by a little white unicorn with a bright yellow spiral horn on its snout. I found it quite amusing and we both urged Kathleen to climb aboard and go for a ride. It was a chance to be a little silly and create a memorable photo opportunity. Once aboard the unicorn, Kathleen raised her purse above her head and began to swing it like a rodeo lasso. Izzy palmed her phone and set it to selfie mode with the three of us making ridiculous poses and donning childlike facial expressions. After the allotted time had expired and the unicorn ceased its gallop, we began to review the photos and share laugh after laugh.

"I'm definitely sending these to Micro" she said.

"Send them to me too" said Izzy. "These are hilarious."

"Ok. Doing it now. Hey, wait a minute. Look at this!"

A closer look at the photo showed part of the store's interior and captured a slim man putting an object inside of his jacket. Curiosity immediately invited us to stay and witness the outcome, but Kathleen received a text message stating that her patient's treatment was done and to meet him and the specialist in the front lobby area of the hospital. I rubbed my right hand across the nose of the unicorn for good luck. Our destination was directly across the street and adjacent to it was the parking lot. We hurried across the busy city street, dodging text-messaging drivers and yellow cabs who had activated their off-duty signs, deterring us from flagging them down.

Izzy offered to retrieve the car from the parking lot and bring it around to the front, whilst Kathleen connected with her client and spoke with the specialist. Following hospital protocol, she gathered his belongings and wheeled him through the sliding double doors, down the access ramp and onto the sidewalk pick-up area. As we rounded the final curve before reaching the sidewalk pick-up area, I made a comment to Izzy about how narrow the driving space was and that he needed the precision of a surgeon to maneuver through. He agreed. With the assistance of the curbside valet, we positioned the transport van with the opening towards the street as it would give us more room to operate. I found it a bit unusual to expose the loading pedestrians to oncoming traffic, but this was New York City and it is infamous for its state of mind. Kathleen entered the passenger side door as the valet guided the man in the wheelchair to the side entrance. Manners instructed Izzy to run around the front side of the van to offer some assistance and when the man stood up to greet him, they both locked eyes and stood deadlocked in agonizing pain. Before a word could be spoken, we heard a shout coming from the direction of the little convenience store,

"Stop! Thief! Stop!"

The front door of the convenience store flew open and the slim man who had been captured in our unicorn photos bolted from obscurity and into the bright lights of Manhattan. Running in a zig zag type of pattern, he pressed his left arm tightly against his midsection, securing his item from slipping from his grasp. Attempting to make a blended getaway onto the crowded street, the perpetrator hopped over a parked car and landed in the path of an oncoming vehicle. The inattentive driver lifted her head and became startled upon seeing a man suddenly appear from thin air. She violently jolted the steering wheel, causing the car to swerve just enough to avoid hitting this pedestrian but her unusual maneuver at a high rate of speed placed her vehicle into the path of the two stonewalled men. The vehicle collided with Kathleen's client, hurling him twenty-five feet in the air and crash landing on top of the ghostly-white unicorn.

Immediately, the surrounding air became overwhelmed with patronizing gasps and sympathetic sighs. Kathleen ran to the aid of her client, followed by some alerted hospital staff and the horde of innocent bystanders. I looked at Izzy in disbelief and took off running towards the convenience store. Parting my way through the crowd, I stood over Kathleen's shoulder and peered directly into the face of the injured party. As the hospital EMT staff attempted to control the scene, I further noticed that the horn of the unicorn had pierced through the victim's body and he was losing consciousness. I felt a cold presence appear behind me filled with animosity and disdain. I was shocked as I realized why we both recognized that face. The man whispered something in Kathleen's ear and she turned and looked up in our direction. All the fragmented conversations taking place within the crowd gave way to coveted silence and a direct line of communication between the man standing behind me and the man laying before me, and before losing consciousness, the victim managed to murmur,

"Izzy...

Izz, please don't...

Please Israel...

Please forgive me."

From over my right shoulder, a leather jacket and matching hat fell just beyond the base of the unicorn atop a metal trash can. The man standing behind me opened his right hand, releasing the tight grip of the little boy's hand, allowing him to walk away forever. I gave my friend a hug and patted him on the back. His tears fell onto my shoulder, cleansing himself from all of the toxic impurities that were contaminating his soul. With the his heartbeat returning to normal, he replied,

"I forgive you."

Later that evening in the emergency lobby of the hospital, we awaited the final news from the surgeon. No one said a word. Kathleen's facial expressions told me that she was still trying to put the puzzle pieces in place and was looking for me to issue her a lifeline to find the answer. I turned my attention towards the television as a late breaking newsflash had just appeared across the screen:

"This just in. A tragic accident occurred in front of New York Hospital this evening. Our sources confirm that a man in a wheelchair was fatally injured after being struck by an out-of-control vehicle that propelled him into the air and onto the sharp edges of a fictional carousel character. We learned that the victim had just received medical treatment at the hospital and was being loaded into a transport vehicle when another unidentified man, who had just burglarized the convenience store directly

across the street, tried to escape by leaping over a parked car and into the path of oncoming traffic. The driver managed to elude the culprit, but in doing so, lost control of her vehicle and fatally struck the victim. Surveillance footage from inside the convenience store captured a glimpse of the perpetrator's face and his dark sweatshirt with the letters D.I.P.U.T.S. Police believe that this individual may also have a connection with a fatal subway shooting that claimed the life of a young man a few months earlier. If you know the whereabouts of this individual or have any information, please call

*crime stoppers at **1-800-4DIPUTS**."*

DEDICATED TO:

MY MOTHER FOR HER UNCONDITIONAL LOVE AND SUPPORT AND FOR THE EXTREMELY HARD AND EMOTIONAL DECISIONS; MY FATHER FOR NEVER GIVING UP

TO CONNIE AND LAURA BECK FOR OPENING UP YOUR HEARTS AND ALLOWING ME TO BECOME A PART OF YOUR FAMILY;

THANK YOU TO:

TO MY WIFE AND KIDS – NOTHING IS OR WILL EVER BE MORE IMPORTANT TO ME THAN YOU

MR. DARREN E. JOHNSON FOR GIVING ME THE COURAGE TO WRITE;
THE FRESH AIR FUND & QUEENSBRIDGE HOUSES/JACOB RIIS COMMUNITY CENTER;
MY ENTIRE EXTENDED FAMILY-
(COLEMAN/WARD/DENTON/GAYMON/HAYES/JACKSON/HASLIPS);
MR. LOU GARNES, MR. STEPHEN SKIPPER & ALL MY ST. RITA TEAMMATES
MS. NOLA HAMILTON & THE ROBINSONS
THE CARUFE FAMILY FOR STEPPING UP AND MAKING A HUGE DIFFERENCE
THE FEILER FAMILY

RESTING BUT NEVER FORGOTTEN:

JAMES & NETTIE WARD, ALICE COLEMAN, RUTH GAYMON, LORENZO WARD, SALANA RYANT, BETTY WARD, JOHN HICKS JR & SR, DIAHANN HICKS, WILLIAM WARD, JOSIE HASLIP, THE NESSLES,
BILL & CHRISTINE JOHNSON, RAY & MABEL DUNN, BOB WELCH, JERRY SIMMONS, DERRICK GILMORE, WARREN 'WEE-WOP' WALKER, WINSTON NICHOLAS

www.ingramcontent.com/pod-product-compliance
Lightning Source LLC
Chambersburg PA
CBHW060922180626
46817CB00004B/1348